Bending his head, Zaire feathered kisses onto China's cheeks, moving down to her lower lip. His taunting tongue teased her mouth, until she opened up for it to enter. The next several kisses were light and playful.

As the kiss grew hotter with passion, China found it hard to keep from squirming. Her body was on fire from Zaire's burning touch. They'd come so close to making love earlier, but it hadn't happened.

Lying flat on his back, Zaire rolled China over until she was on top of him. Wrapping her up in his arms, he kissed her passionately. Slightly loosening his grip on her, his hand roved the back of her thighs with tenderness.

Prompted by his nearly out-of-control desire, Zaire took his explorations further, slipping his hand under China's dress and caressing her silk-clad rear. Feeling the prickly heat of her flesh through her panties, his one desperate desire was to cool down her body—and heat it right back up, over and over again.

Books by Linda Hudson-Smith

Kimani Romance

Forsaking All Others
Indiscriminate Attraction
Romancing the Runway
Destiny Calls
Kissed by a Carrington
Promises to Keep
Seduction at Whispering Lakes

LINDA HUDSON-SMITH

was born in Canonsburgh, Pennsylvania, and raised in Washington, Pennsylvania. She furthered her educational goals by attending Duff's Business Institute, Pittsburgh, Pennsylvania. The mother of two sons, Linda resides with her husband, Rudy, in League City, Texas.

After illness forced her to leave a successful marketing and public relations career in 1991, Linda turned to writing as a creative outlet. Dedicated to inspire readers to overcome adversity against all odds, she has published twenty-nine acclaimed novels to date. During Harlequin's 60th Anniversary party held in Washington, D.C., Linda received an award for her twenty-fifth published novel. Linda is an *Essence* bestselling author.

Since 2001 Linda has served as a national spokesperson and a staunch advocate for the Lupus Foundation of America. She travels around the country delivering inspirational messages of hope. In 2002 her Lupus Awareness Campaign was a major part of her book tour to Germany, where she visited numerous military bases. Linda is an active supporter of the NAACP and American Cancer Society. She is also a member of Romance Writers of America and Black Writers Alliance.

To find out more about Linda Hudson-Smith, please visit her website at www.lindahudsonsmith.com.

SEDUCTION
AT
WHISPERING
Lakes

LINDA HUDSON-SMITH

KIMANI
ROMANCE

This novel is dedicated to
Farzaneh Banki, M.D.
Thank you so much for taking such special care of me
during the most difficult time in my life.
Allowing God to work through you and your gifted hands
saved my life. I will always be grateful to the
wonderful person and physician you are.
God Bless You Always

KIMANI PRESS™

ISBN-13: 978-0-373-86230-6

Recycling programs
for this product may
not exist in your area.

SEDUCTION AT WHISPERING LAKES

www.kimanipress.com

Printed in U.S.A.

Dear Reader,

I sincerely hope you enjoy reading *Seduction at Whispering Lakes,* my latest love story featuring China Braxton, R.N., and Zaire Kingdom, owner of Whispering Lakes Ranch, a huge Texas spread offering ranch-style living and a variety of fun country-western events for guests of all ages to enjoy.

An immediate attraction sparks between China and Zaire. As they get to know each other, readers can join them on an adventurous journey. As China learns how life is lived on a dude ranch, she often compares the ranch style of living to living in Los Angeles, her native home.

I am very interested in hearing your comments and thoughts about this story. Please enclose a self-addressed, stamped envelope and all your contact information in mail to Linda Hudson-Smith, 16516 El Camino Real, Box 174, Houston, TX 77062. You can also email your comments to lindahudsonsmith@yahoo.com. Please visit my website and fill out my contact form at www.lindahudsonsmith.com. I am also on www.facebook.com.

Enjoy,

Linda Hudson-Smith

Chapter 1

Pride filled Zaire Kingdom as he sat atop powerful Thunder, one of the most beautiful palominos out of his stable of numerous horses. His golden brown eyes stared down at the magnificent ranch below, as the orange sun slowly descended. The vast acreage where hilly land masses and skies appeared to meet was a sight to behold. The view from the highest ridge on the Brownsville, Texas, property was breathtaking. This was his home.

Several of the nine beautiful lakes on Whispering Lakes Ranch offered great fishing experiences, one of Zaire's favorite pastimes. The entire place was a relaxation haven for the successful corporate cowboy and his host of family members.

Zaire's eyes suddenly zeroed in on a car pulled off to the side of the road leading up to the main building where guests registered to check into the log cabin–style guest cottages. Spotting a slender figure standing next to the auto, it appeared to be a woman, but he was too far away to be certain. Why the driver had pulled over was his main concern. Guests didn't normally check in this late in the day. He wondered if the car or possibly the driver was in distress. Either way, help was on the way.

Pulling gently on the reins, turning Thunder around, Zaire headed in the direction of the automobile. With the horse's hoofs flying across the familiar terrain, Zaire felt totally relaxed in the saddle, loving the feel of the wind. Out of the many entertainment venues offered at the ranch, he loved riding his horses and teaching his guests how to ride.

Stopping Thunder a couple of feet away from the car, Zaire dismounted. Tethering the reins to a nearby fence, he walked over to where a young woman leaned against the driver's door of a late-model Toyota convertible. An expression of total bewilderment was etched on her pretty face. "Is everything okay, Ma'am?"

Embarrassment flashing in her sparkling chocolate brown eyes, China Braxton looked up at Zaire. "Would you believe I'm lost?"

"That's not so hard to believe." Zaire chuckled. "Where you headed?"

"Whispering Lakes Ranch. I have reservations there. Think you can point a lost city girl in the right direction?"

Zaire grinned. "You're already on the ranch." He pointed ahead. "Another mile or so up the road is the registration building. I'll lead the way on horseback."

China sighed with relief. "That's so kind. Are you a guest, too?"

"You could say that." He was a permanent guest, but she'd find it out in due time.

"My dad told me a lot about this place. I hope it lives up to all his hype. By the way, I'm China Braxton." Looking over at the horse, she wished she had the nerve to stroke it. Being intimidated by such a powerful, beautiful animal made her feel silly.

"I'm Zaire Kingdom, Ma'am." He gave her a warm smile. "Ready?"

"Lead the way."

Waiting until China was buckled up, Zaire mounted Thunder. Settling into a moderately paced gallop, he rode toward the main building. The area would be well lit in another couple of yards. She would've seen the huge neon sign welcoming guests to the property had she continued on. He gave thought to adding an additional mile or two of lights to the route, yet no previous problems with lighting had been reported.

Even though Thunder wouldn't stray far from its owner, Zaire tethered his horse. Bred, born and raised on this land, Thunder knew every square inch of the entire ranch.

China looked toward the massive A-frame structure. Turning around, she faced Zaire. "Impressive piece of architecture! Wish I'd gotten here a long time ago. I stopped in town 'cause I can't resist browsing quaint little gift shops. Billboard advertisings are posted everywhere. Do you think someone's inside to check me in?"

He gave an assuring smile. "Don't worry. You'll be checked in. Come with me."

China lifted an eyebrow. "You seem to know the ropes around here."

"You could say that," he answered.

China followed Zaire into the cozy, comfortably furnished lobby. A beautiful pregnant woman with flawless burnished brown skin stood behind the counter. As she looked up, her striking, dark amber eyes showed compassion. Flowing like a curtain of silk, thick auburn hair fell softly below the stunning woman's slender shoulders.

"China Braxton, this is Hailey Hamilton-Kingdom. She'll get you checked in and assigned to a cabin."

Acknowledging each other with slight nods, the women smiled warmly.

"I'll wait around and escort you to the cabin," Zaire said. "The property is well lit, but I'm sure you can use help with your luggage."

"Thank you." China was a bit amazed by this good-looking man. He reminded her of her father, a loving, caring gentleman from head to toe. Brody Braxton had always been ready and willing to help anyone in need.

"I'll be right outside when you finish up. Take your time, China," Zaire said.

China's eyes followed Zaire to the door. Knowing she'd see him again made her smile. As of late, she hadn't met many kindhearted men. His left ring finger was bare, she'd noted, but Hailey's last name was also Kingdom. *Was she his wife?*

Hailey pushed a lengthy form in front of China. "Please read the rental agreement and sign at the bottom. We're thrilled to have you as a guest. Welcome!"

"I'm excited to be here. My father loved this place." At the thought of Brody Braxton, her eyes suddenly filled with tears. "He requested I bring him back here to scatter his ashes. A native Texan, Dad chose Whispering Lakes Ranch as his final resting place."

Hailey felt instant sympathy for China, but she didn't think now was the time to address the obvious grief.

"Do you work here full-time?" China asked Hailey, shaking off her grief.

"I help out whenever and wherever. I'm on maternity leave from the Air Force. Not sure yet if I'll return to active duty after the baby comes. We'll see."

"Is Zaire an employee? He seems so knowledgeable

about the place." Talking about Zaire would be a good distraction from her father.

Hailey laughed softly. "Along with his brothers, Zurich and Zane, the three Kingdom brothers own this fantastic resort. Zaire gave up his corporate job to live his dream. He's made the ranch a favorite vacation spot for folks from all over the world."

China smiled softly. "Three *Z*'s, huh!"

"Their mom loved the names. My mother-in-law, Bernice, is a sweetheart. So is my father-in-law, Morgan."

"Wow, you sound like a woman who actually likes her in-laws! Which brother are you married to?" Hoping she wasn't married to Zaire, China sucked in a deep breath, holding it tightly.

"Zurich. He's retired from the Air Force. He's employed at a local Brownsville television station. We're both meteorologists." Hailey grinned. "I need to make a slight correction to your comment. I love my in-laws. They're wonderful."

China was pleased at Hailey's answer. "Do your in-laws visit the ranch often?"

"They own a house on the land and a huge motor home. The entire family has custom-built homes on Whispering Lakes Ranch. Our residences are a good distance apart, but we're as close as a phone call. Our family participates in most of the guest activities. The brothers and their father pull many of the instructor and guide duties."

China signed the registration form and handed it back to Hailey along with her American Express card. "Do you need any ID?"

"Just your driver's license. The other important information was supplied on the application you filled out online."

Amazed by the wealth of information Hailey had imparted on the Kingdom family, China had an urge to ask her if Zaire was married. She refrained. Instead, she picked up a brochure describing the ranch, though she had glanced over one at home.

The dude-style ranch was advertised as a lively playground for family vacationers and couples or singles looking for a fun getaway. Horseback/trail riding, hiking, calf roping, swimming, fishing, tossing horseshoes, Country-Western dancing and having fun barbecues were a big part of the ranch's entertainment package. Inside a barnlike structure, the indoor-activities clubhouse included a bar, dance floor, pool tables and mechanical bull. Karaoke was offered two nights a week. Weekends featured live bands.

Whispering Lakes Ranch was touted as the perfect place for the outdoorsman or the sports-minded woman, as well as for the man or woman who blossomed outdoors in the wide-open spaces. China was glad she'd get to experience firsthand the place that had kept her father intrigued enough to return there year after year. Working long hours and continuing education classes had kept her from vacationing with Brody.

Chewing on a toothpick, Zaire looked out over the horizon. He never got enough of this idyllic place. His love of the land and the peace it brought was why he'd left his corporate job. He'd leave the hustle and bustle of city life every weekend and on holidays to ride the range, survey and explore the extensive Kingdom-owned acreage.

The more Zaire had thought about what he could possibly do with all this prime land he and his brothers owned, the more elaborate plans began forming in his mind. After several months of serious soul-searching and researching, he'd shared his ideas with his brothers. Sold on Zaire's brilliant vision, they'd agreed to act upon it. Zurich and Zane hadn't initially planned to live on the land like Zaire had. The brothers later realized it was the best solution for making the place a huge success.

In perfect harmony with the land, Zaire was never more content in his life. From sunup to sundown, he lived and breathed Whispering Lakes Ranch. This was his safe haven, a place that never let him down. He had no desire to live anywhere else.

Hearing the door open and shut, Zaire turned around and saw China. "I'll drive my SUV back to the cottages. You can follow me. What cabin did Hailey assign you?"

China looked at the key in her hand. "Cabin nine."

Zaire nodded to show he approved. "The full kitchen and separate rooms make it one of our premier cottages. I think you'll love it. Wait here until I pull around the SUV."

As Zaire strode toward the side of the building, China took in an eyeful. Watching him walk was electrifying. The man was over six feet tall, deliciously dark and handsome. She loved his sexy, confident swagger. The cowboy boots appeared to be cut from the finest leather. The off-white Stetson with a thin black leather band further enhanced his hot, rancher-cowboy aura. If she lit a match right now, his white-hot sex appeal would no doubt spark a blazing fire.

Zaire wasn't a bit surprised by the amount of luggage China had. He hadn't helped out many women who hadn't brought along every single creature comfort, those least needed on the open range. Jeans, T-shirts, shorts, tennis shoes, hiking boots, swimwear and a few dresses for special events would suffice.

As Zaire stored the luggage in the roomy walk-in closet, the audible gasps from China weren't lost on him. This was one of the best cabins at the resort. He couldn't hold back his laughter, as she dared to bounce up and down on the queen-size bed like a child. The bed was beautifully dressed in a box-stitched white comforter, white sheets and pillowcases and frilly pillow shams. A variety of brightly colored pillows breathed life into the snowy white linens.

China pointed at the windows. "I really like the wood shutters, and the off-white rocker-recliner looks pretty comfy. Does the fireplace burn wood or gas?"

"It's electric. With a flick of the switch it can produce heat and display colorful mock flames. Most guests only use heat in winter months, but almost everyone uses it for atmosphere. Can I get you anything before I leave?"

Frowning, she palmed her forehead. "I forgot to get a couple of Diet Cokes from the vending machine. I can do without until tomorrow. No big deal."

Zaire steered her back to the kitchen and opened the full-size refrigerator door. "All sorts of soft drinks are in here." He picked up a form. "Whatever you use, check it off on here. You'll be billed at checkout. Soft drinks are much cheaper here than those in other hotel vending machines."

He then showed her the cupboard where microwavable cups of soup, popcorn, chips, single-serving-size cereals, packaged pastries, candy bars and a variety of other food items and treats were stored. The kitchen was equipped with modern appliances.

"How often are perishable items changed out?"

"Most food items have expiration dates. Our employees check the refrigerator and pantry often. Small cartons of milk are changed out daily."

China laughed. "I'm sorry. I didn't mean to imply anything sinister. I'm terribly curious by nature. I'm a nurse so I always concern myself with health-and-safety issues."

"A nurse, huh? Well, the closest medical facility is twenty miles away. We've thought of hiring a full-time RN, but we haven't had enough incidents of illness or injury to warrant it. As well as staff members, our lifeguards are certified in CPR and first aid. We also supply transportation to and from the medical facility."

The expression on China's face showed amazement. "You Kingdom brothers got it going on. I'm looking forward to my stay."

"We're happy to have you. If you're not interested in cooking, breakfast is served in the dining room of the main building from five-thirty to ten-thirty. Look at the activity schedule for whatever you're interested in. There's plenty to do out here."

"I recall reading an endless list of activities. I want to go fishing and learn to ride a horse, but I'm a bit intimidated by their size. Your horse is one big boy."

"Thunder *is* gigantic but gentle as a lamb. Let me know when you're ready to get acquainted with him. Fishing excursions begin at five o'clock."

A gasp was followed by a loud groan from China. "Why so early?"

"The fish are hungry and biting." He moved toward the door. "I'd better get going. See you around. Have a great evening, China."

"You, too, Zaire. Thanks for everything, especially for rescuing me."

He grinned. "Glad I could be of service." Backing out of the exit, he closed the door behind him. Turning around again, he rapped hard on her door.

China appeared immediately. "Did you forget something?"

"Not really. Wanted to tell you since it is Friday, there's a great band playing tonight in the pavilion, which also serves as a clubhouse, bandstand and dance hall." He looked down at his watch and whistled. "The band starts in a couple of hours."

"I think I *will* check out the band. I probably won't get

there at starting time, though. A shower and short nap will help rejuvenate me. Will you be there?"

"The entire Kingdom family will be there. We pretty much check in on everything happening around the place. I rarely stay until the last set, but I'll definitely drop in."

Resisting a strong urge to flirt with Zaire, China smiled. "Good. Hope to see you there." China wished her lifelong best friend, Brooke Clay, had come to keep her in line.

Zaire grinned. "You probably will. Get settled in. Later, China."

Hearing the door close, she crossed her arms, rubbing them up and down. Zaire unsettled her in the strangest way. Her wild attraction to him was crazy. Walking around the cabin, familiarizing herself with the surroundings, she was pleased with everything.

Along with washcloths and hand linens, large, thirsty white bath towels were stacked on a rack above the bathroom sink. A hair dryer was mounted on a wall. Complimentary toiletry items, nestled in a decorative gold wire basket, were set out on the ceramic tile counter. A shower cap, shoe shine and a mini sewing kit were included.

The Jacuzzi caused her to change her mind about showering. Relaxing in a tub was more appealing. Turning on the faucets, she fiddled with the dials until the water temperature was right. After filling the tub to where it was safe to turn on the jets, she rushed back to her unpacked suitcases. Opening the smaller case that held aromatherapy products, she quickly chose lavender oil and hurried back to the bathroom, eager to enjoy this soak.

Wrapped up cozily in a thick white velour robe, China lay in the center of the bed, her head propped up on several pillows. Though she felt drowsy, she wanted to read through the ranch brochures before taking a brief nap. Next

to the numerous offerings of supervised activities, the instructors' names were listed. Zaire's name appeared on the
schedule quite a bit. The man was busy as a swarm of
worker bees.

The Kingdom brothers had thought of everything when
they'd planned out the ranch. A house of worship was built
next to the main building. A retired clergyman, Pastor
Royal Clark, came from nearby Brownsville to minister
to family and guests.

Checking off each interesting activity, China made sure
to schedule it on Zaire's watch. She liked the thought of
having him as her instructor. The idea of getting to know
him on a personal level appealed to her.

Wearing sexy, formfitting white jeans and a chic
designer mint-green scooped-neck linen top, China looked
like a fresh spring day. Sucking in a deep breath, she
stepped into the cavernous barnlike pavilion. Blaring full-
blast from numerous speakers, DJ-spun music greeted her.
Figuring the band was probably on break, she covered her
ears briefly. Spotting Hailey near the bar, China strolled
in her direction.

As if they were old friends, the two women exchanged
warm pleasantries.

"Glad you came out to join the fun tonight. Zaire told us
you might show up. I'd like you to meet other family members and a few employees. Okay with you?"

China nodded. "My pleasure. I'd love to meet everyone."

Hailey took China by the hand. "Come on. We've got a
great table where we can see everything that goes on. It's
reserved for family and special guests."

Did Hailey consider her a special guest? At any rate, it
was a nice thought. China felt nervous as Hailey introduced
her to tall, dark and gorgeous Zurich. Family resemblances

were striking. Hailey then introduced the family matriarch, her mother-in-law, Bernice Kingdom.

Bernice smiled sweetly. "Welcome to Whispering Lakes Ranch, China. I hope your stay with us is memorable." Bernice turned. "This is my husband, Morgan."

The tall man with a dark brown complexion was good-looking. As she pointed to another male, China could easily see he was another brother. "My son Zane and his girl-friend, Gayle McCray, are high school teachers. They work with the family on weekends during the school year and full-time in the summer. Gayle helps out with arts-and-crafts and fills in wherever else she's needed. She has God-gifted hands."

China shook hands with everyone, flashing a radiant smile.

It hadn't taken China long to notice how stylishly Bernice was dressed. Appearing much younger than her fifty-plus years, she had layered medium-length mixed-gray hair. Sparkling pecan-brown eyes were as pretty as her caramel-brown face.

Three lovely older women joined them. Bernice warmly hugged the ladies, introducing them to China. "Up until I married, my sisters and I lived together."

China greeted the animated ladies, who were as stylish as their sister. She turned to Bernice. "What a wonderful family you have. It's nice to meet each of you."

China's thoughts went to her mother, who had run off with another man when China was a little girl, leaving her father to raise her alone. She still felt that she'd missed out on something wonderful by the absence of a solid family. Having no mother or siblings around had been hard, and, now that her father rested in peace, China felt totally alone in the world.

Sensing China's sadness, Bernice slid her arm around

her shoulders, hugging her in a motherly way. "We'd love for you to join us at our table. But let me warn you. We're a lively bunch, a very vocal one. Our guys can get a bit racy with the jokes."

China laughed. "It sounds exciting. Thank you, Ms. Bernice, for the kind offer. I'd be honored to share the family table."

Painfully aware of Zaire's absence, China recalled him saying he'd drop in at the club later. *Would he be okay with her, a total stranger, joining his family?*

No matter what Zaire thought about the invite, China was glad to have people to share the time with. The Kingdom family seemed to know just how to have fun.

As the band strode onstage to reclaim their places, lights flickered on and off. Patrons enthusiastically applauded their return, thrilled the break was over. Music was immediately cued. Starting out the set with a Country-Western flavor, the band began playing. Dressed in moderately flashy Western attire, a fabulous gray Stetson atop his head, the attractive vocalist stepped to the microphone. Seconds after he sang a few lyrics to the song, China felt the overpowering spirit of his sexy, melodic voice.

Charley Pride was the only other black man China had heard perform in the sultry Country-Western genre. Strumming his guitar like he caressed the softness of a woman, the featured singer had an amazing voice, a distinct CW twang.

A few minutes later China was alone at the table. The family group had rushed onto the dance floor, where they zealously performed the electric slide, CW style. Watching Zaire's mom and aunts moving to the music like teenagers had China joining in on the clapping and wild cheering. These women apparently lived life to the fullest.

"Enjoying yourself?"

The familiar voice made China's heart rate go berserk. She didn't have to look up to see who had spoken. Zaire's memorable, lazy Texas drawl was distinctively white hot and sexy. "I'm having a blast." Hoping he'd sit down, she looked up at him.

Zaire leaned against the sturdy table. Watching his family dancing and having a great time made him feel good. It was hard not to think back on the days when the entire family was in emotional disarray. His mother and her three sons had been verbally and physically abused by her husband, their natural father, Macon Kingdom.

"Looks like they're having a wonderful time," China said, breaking into Zaire's dark thoughts. "Everyone seems so happy."

"You don't have a clue." Zaire's eyes clouded briefly. "Those four sisters are utterly amazing. There's more energy in their baby fingers than most people have in their entire bodies." Zaire chuckled. "You haven't seen the half of it yet. Here they come."

Zaire greeted his mother and each of his aunts. Cheery hellos and tender hugs were passed around. "What can I get my favorite ladies to drink?"

Each woman told Zaire what she wanted. He then asked China her preference. After mentally jotting down the orders, he left the table.

China didn't know why she suddenly felt lonely with so many people around her. She knew Zaire was coming back to the table. *How much longer would he stay?* She hoped he'd stay until she was ready to leave.

Zane kissed Gayle, then stood. "I'm heading to the bar. What about a fresh drink?"

Covering the top of her glass with her hand, Gayle smiled at Zane. "I'm fine for right now, honey."

"Be right back." Leaning down, he kissed her again.

For the next few minutes, China closely watched the loving interactions between the Kingdoms. They really seemed into each other. Like his brothers, she wondered if Zaire also had a special someone. He seemed like such an attentive man.

Quietly observing the happenings around her, China sat contentedly.

Morgan and Bernice's love for each other was transparent. It seemed Zurich and Hailey had long ago gone off the deep end. The couple was obviously madly in love. Each time he reached down and caressed her pregnant stomach, he stroked her with the same kind of loving tenderness China had only experienced from one man—her father.

Zaire returned with a waitress who helped him pass out the drinks. Taking each glass from a metal tray, he set it down in front of the appropriate person. He knew his family like the back of his hand.

Zaire set a can of Diet Coke in front of China then wiped the top with a paper napkin. Seating himself next to her, he quickly popped open the can.

Quite the gentleman, too, she thought. "Thanks. How much do I owe you?"

He gave her a bright smile. "Your sincere *thanks* paid me in full. And you're mighty welcome. Let me know if it's cold enough."

China poured a small amount of liquid into her glass and took a sip. "Ice cold."

"Great. Are you hungry? We serve hot wings, chicken strips, nachos, personal pan-size pizzas, hot dogs, hamburgers and snack items like chips and pretzels."

"I love hot wings, but I can't eat a whole order. Want to share one?"

"My pleasure," he said, grinning broadly. "I'll be right back."

China thought his kindness and thoughtfulness were extraordinary. "I'll be waiting." China and Zaire exchanged flirty looks. By the time he looked away, she felt totally breathless.

Zaire had had a hard time tearing his eyes away from China. The way she'd responded, though nonverbal, had him wondering if she was unattached. A woman so beautiful had to have a man in her life. As a nurse, she probably had a group of doctors and other medical professionals vying for her attention. He couldn't imagine any man not wanting to have her.

Zaire's policy was to never get romantically involved with a guest. His brothers thought his policy on romantic involvements was a stupid one, especially since he spent the majority of his time on the ranch. Single women who were there for vacation normally came in groups. China was the first one he'd known to come alone.

Zaire reminded himself that he'd had his fill of single women, especially those who were untrustworthy.

Chapter 2

Stopping dead in his tracks, Zaire's eyes zeroed in on China out on the dance floor with his mother and three aunts. The ladies had her turning and twisting every which way, teaching her one of several CW line dances they loved.

All Zaire could do was stand there and stare. China was mesmerizing. Her gyrating hips held him spellbound. Imagining her dancing in the nude for him was one of the craziest thoughts he'd had in a long time. It was as delicious as it was insane.

Stepping up to his younger brother, Zurich noticed the questioning look on his face. He then removed from Zaire's hand the tray of food orders. "You were about to drop this. You look like you've been struck by lightning. Pretty little filly, isn't she?"

Acting as if he didn't know what Zurich was talking about, Zaire shrugged, knowing exactly what his brother meant. China was more than just a pretty face. He didn't know how he knew, but he felt confident that there was more to her than a fabulous body and a lovely face, more than what the naked eye could see.

Rarely was Zaire solely attracted to looks. Beauty was skin-deep and only in the eyes of the beholder. A woman's character and spiritual makeup was more important. Somehow, he believed China's moral fiber was above reproach. As for spiritual makeup, it was like God had steered one of His angels onto Whispering Lakes Ranch.

What was happening to him? Zaire wondered why he was so nervous.

While he had no idea what had taken him over, he thought it may be worth exploring, investigating every aspect of a possible miracle visiting his life. As he sat back down to wait for China's return, the overwhelming enthusiasm he felt was foreign. In the next instant, he thought he had gone nuts.

Zaire Kingdom didn't like dwelling on his state of utter loneliness. It didn't do him any good to constantly think about it, yet he'd often admitted it to himself. Even though Zurich was right there and other family members were always near, Zaire was lonesome for a beautiful woman like China. To distract himself, he made small talk with his brothers.

Seeing the group of females coming toward them, Zurich got to his feet.

"You and Hailey are staying, right?" Zaire asked Zurich.

"Of course. We'll be back in just a few minutes." Zurich squeezed Zaire's shoulder. Nodding at China, the eldest brother went off to meet his wife.

Picking up plastic plates and utensils, Zaire set the disposable dinnerware in front of China. "Mind if I fix your plate?"

Smiling, China nodded. "Please do. It's not often I get waited on."

"My pleasure." He put several hot wings onto her plate. He'd had the chef throw together a small portion of potato salad, which wasn't on the club's menu.

"Onion rings or French fries?"

"French fries please." Picking up a wing, China bit right into it. She started gagging. "Water—" she sputtered "—cold water!"

Zaire laughed inwardly. Having anticipated a reaction to the fire-breathing wings, he reached down beside him and retrieved a bottle of cold water. Twisting off the cap, he handed it over to her. "Here you go, China."

Showing her gratitude with a smile, she tossed back the water like it was a lifesaver, draining nearly a quarter of the bottle in one huge gulp. Then she turned narrowed eyes on Zaire. "You knew this would happen, didn't you?"

Zaire threw up his hands. "Guilty as charged. The chicken is hotter than what's served in most places, so I brought you plenty of cold water. Sorry I didn't warn you."

"No, you're not. Those smirking eyes of yours tell a totally different story. You got one over on me. Just remember I owe you one."

Recalling a similar experience Zurich had had with Hailey when they'd first met, Zaire laughed. "You got me. But I took care of you, didn't I?"

"Yeah, you did. You might want to tell the chef to lighten up on the spices. I'm pretty sure my tongue is badly scorched."

"You'll have to tell Bernice Kingdom her wings are too hot. I'm not going there. If I said something, she'd just say 'don't eat them.'"

China grinned. "Okay, so I won't say anything. They *are* good, once you get past the burning sensations. I'll take my time eating the rest."

It was still dark as China made her way to the main building to meet with other guests who'd signed up for the fishing trip. She had given herself so many reasons to just lie there in bed, especially after the long drive from L.A. She hadn't come here to sleep. Her desire to experience the joys her father had felt on this ranch outweighed any excuse she could come up with.

China had, stowed away in her tote bag, an urn filled with Brody's ashes to sprinkle over the lakes. Her father had wanted his remains scattered in several key spots on the ranch. Whispering Lake, the ranch's namesake, was one place.

Dressed in the type of comfortable clothing and footgear the brochure had recommended, China parked the car and cut the engine. Warm, swirling winds hit her head-on as she stepped out of the car. Instead of setting the car's overly sensitive alarm, she made sure all doors were locked.

Surprised to see so many people already in the lobby, China found a seat to wait for further instructions. She had wondered how many guests had signed up for such an early morning outdoor activity. Now she had the answer.

"Hello, dear! I'm Marilee Cotton. All ready for the fishing trip?"

China smiled at the elderly woman with fawn-brown eyes, medium-beige complexion and mixed gray hair. "As ready as I can be. I haven't fished since I was a teenager. I hope this trip will bring back fond memories of when my father took me."

The lady reached over and gently patted China's hand. "It will. Fishing is relaxing and fun, even if you don't catch anything. I'm a resident of Scottsdale, Arizona. What's your name and where do you live?"

"China Braxton, a native resident of Los Angeles, California."

"We're practically neighbors. I fly to L.A. a couple of times a year to lie on the beaches and shop on Rodeo Drive. My husband, Harry, died last year, but I still do everything we did before he fell ill. He wanted me to continue living an active life."

"Good for you, Ms. Marilee," China praised. "I'm sorry for your loss. My father passed away a few weeks ago." She then explained her mission.

Marilee's eyes glowed with sympathy. "Your profound loss is so new. I'm sorry for you. I have warm, wonderful memories to keep me company. Harry and I were so in love. As world travelers, Paris was our favorite European city. We honeymooned there."

"Paris is a top spot on my future traveling agenda." She had a strong urge to hug this dear, sweet lady, but instead she patted her hand in the same comforting way Marilee had touched hers. "How many times have you visited this ranch?"

"Oh, I've lost count. We'd come here for a week and then move up to South Padre Island. We did this every year after the ranch first opened, doing whatever our moods dictated. Harry and I were married for forty-plus years. Do you plan to visit South Padre Island? It's a lovely coastal area on the Gulf of Mexico. Its beaches are beautiful, and the shopping villages are fantastic bargain havens."

China's eyes lit up with recollection. "I saw a day trip featured in one of the brochures. I think I'd like to check it out. Are you taking the excursion?"

"Absolutely! The tour is only offered on Fridays. I'm already signed up. It's another early morning wake-up call, but that's par for the course around here."

"I'll check to see if any seats are left. Perhaps we could sit together," China suggested, feeling good about this kind lady. If she'd been married over forty years, she was probably in her sixties.

Marilee smiled warmly. "I'd love it. You remind me of my daughter Shannon. You both are pretty as a picture. She and her family travel with me as much as possible, although the grandchildren are grown. Glynnis is a recent college graduate, and Steven is a computer specialist."

"May I have everyone's attention?" a deep voice said, quieting all conversation.

The deep, velvety voice caused China's pulse rate to race. As she looked at Zaire, warmth flooded through her. Corporate cowboy was a befitting moniker for him. His black jeans were creased to perfection. An off-white Western-style shirt showcased his broad shoulders and bulging upper muscles. His thighs appeared powerful. Riding Thunder was probably responsible for the lower portion of his physique. This was the first time China had seen him without a hat, but a Stetson was in his hand. His dark hair was cut low and neatly edged.

"Because we have so many guests signed up for the fishing trip, we'll be using two guides. My brother Zane will take one group, and I'll handle the other. We'll be fishing on two lakes that are side-by-side. The first group of names I call will go with me. The rest of this group can follow Zane."

Zaire called out several names. China hated that hers wasn't among them. He then called for Marilee Cotton. Those already there when China had arrived were obviously being called first. She'd actually thought she might be only one of a handful of people up and out this early. She'd been dead wrong.

"That's it for my list," Zaire announced. "Zane will take care of the rest of you. The vans are outside. We'll board fishing boats once we get to the lakes."

China could literally taste her disappointment. It was bitter.

Marilee got to her feet. Bending down, she gave her new friend a quick hug.

"Sorry we won't be together. Perhaps we'll get another opportunity. Maybe we can chat over breakfast or lunch one day. South Padre Island is still a prospect."

"It certainly is. Have a good time, Ms. Marilee. I'll see you at the lake."

China grabbed her tote and headed for the door to meet with Zane's group. Two vans were lined up at the front entrance. As she walked over to the vehicle, China heard her name called. Turning around, she saw Marilee summoning her.

Smiling broadly, Marilee grabbed China by the hand. "You can ride with me. This nice gentleman, Mr. Wilson Vanderbilt, has agreed to swap vans."

China wondered if anyone could hear the melody breaking out in her heart. Although she could fantasize about Zaire becoming her lover, she really wanted his friendship. Enchanted by the way he carried himself, she felt sure he was a decent, honorable man. China could easily admit to liking Zaire.

Zaire helped the women maneuver the steps up into the van. Smiling at China, he took hold of her hand. "It seems you've made a fast friend in Mrs. Cotton. I overheard her plea for Mr. Vanderbilt to change vans so you two could ride together. I hope the arrangements are agreeable."

You have no idea how agreeable. China smiled sweetly.

"Mrs. Cotton and I have discovered a few things in common despite our age difference. I'm pleased."

Zaire grinned. "That's the kind of stuff we love to hear. We want our guests to be one hundred percent happy and content."

China nodded. "This guest is both. Thanks for caring enough to ask."

Smiling, Zaire tipped his hat and moved away.

It didn't surprise Zaire that China wasn't the least bit squeamish about baiting her hook with a slimy, wiggly worm. As a nurse, she'd probably seen more than her fair share of gory things. She was good at obeying orders and executing everything he'd instructed her to do—and without question. He liked how eagerly she fully engaged in the activities. China was a woman who seemed to have the same amount of zest for life as the highly active females in his family.

Many of the folks in the boat Zaire commandeered were quiet and still a tad sleepy. Once rods were cast, folks seemed perfectly willing to keep a close eye on their fishing lines. The atmosphere was peaceful as a bright yellow sun ascended.

From the first moment China felt a tug on her line, her excited yelps completely disrupted the quietness. "I've got something, Ms. Marilee," she shouted. Looking at Zaire, she appeared hopeful. "Do you think it's a fish?"

"Let's hope so." Zaire knew the tugging on the line could be a result of several things but had no desire to dampen China's spirit. Her wide and bright smile was engaging. Seeing her looking so happy did his heart good.

"It's getting stronger," she yelled. "Please help me. I don't want to lose it."

The lake was kept stocked with a variety of fish. Catfish, a favorite delight in these parts, were abundant. For China's pleasure, Zaire hoped she had a great catch and not a discarded item, like an old shoe.

China's struggle with the line increased, growing more intense. Zaire came up behind her. Covering her hands with his, he added the extra strength needed to land the catch. She was suddenly propelled back into him and his lower anatomy responded immediately.

Avoiding China's hips, Zaire continued to help reel in the catch. Upon revealing her grand prize, a beautiful striped bass, everyone clapped. Cheering and laughter rent the air. No sooner had the day's first catch been taken off the hook than another fisherman yelped excitedly, telling the others about a strong tugging on the line.

In a helter-skelter manner Zaire moved from one guest to the next, helping each person reel in their prize catch. The experienced fishermen also jumped in to help out folks new to the sport. The large boat rocked but was in no danger of tipping over.

The kids' reaction to their catches was what Zaire enjoyed most. The encouraging hugs they received from parents, especially dads, caused Zaire to wonder if he'd ever have a child of his own. The girls on the Little League baseball and Pop Warner football teams he had the pleasure of coaching were nothing short of amazing dynamos. Coaching the kids brought the greatest pleasure to the Kingdom brothers, who loved working with children because of their own abusive childhoods.

China was tickled silly to see Ms. Marilee and Mr. Vanderbilt seated on the grass lakeside, sharing a meal from provided box lunches. The lady was smiling brightly, and a lot. The two appeared pretty close in age. *Could this be a love connection?* Instead of intruding upon what appeared to be a personal discussion, China claimed a patch of grass a few feet away from the elderly couple.

The vans would return to the ranch once lunch was over. At two o'clock China had scheduled a horseback riding lesson. Zaire was the instructor. She feared making a fool of herself since she was intimidated by the big but beautiful beasts. For her, since the death of her father, conquering all her fears was important. She didn't want to live out life fearful of anything.

Walking over to China, Zaire dropped down on the grassy knoll. Positive she reeked of raw fish, China felt uncomfortable having him in such close proximity. She had used sanitizing wipes to take care of her hands, but she still felt self-conscious.

Zaire grinned. "Congratulations! Not only did you land the largest fish, you caught the most. Five fish is a pretty good haul for someone who hasn't fished in a long time. Your two rainbow trout are beauties."

China giggled. "Who would've ever thought it? I regret not coming here to the ranch with Dad. He invited me numerous times, but I always had work. So far, it's been a fun adventure. I'm sorry I missed out on the memories we could've made. But I've definitely earned bragging rights on the number of fish I caught. I bet your mother and aunts are good at fishing."

"You got that right! They love to fish. Mom cleans all the catches, freezing what she doesn't cook up right away. As for your dad, he has a lot to be proud of."

"Thank you. Speaking of dads, yours seems pretty proud of his three guys. He's lively, too, with his silky-smooth moves. Your parents dance well together. I guess rhythm and harmony are what happens when you've been married a long time."

Looking right into China's face, Zaire shrugged. "I guess

five years is a long time to be married, especially by today's standards."

China appeared totally perplexed. "Five years? I don't think I understand."

"Morgan Cobb is our stepfather, a good friend of our own father. At first, we didn't like him because he knew Dad was abusing his family. None of us understood why he'd hang out with an evil man like Macon if he wasn't the same kind of man."

China's eyes softened. "Birds of a feather don't always flock together, Zaire."

Agreeing with her, he nodded. "You're right. That's the same thing Hailey told Zurich when he first voiced his negative feelings about Morgan to her."

Briefly, China touched Zaire's hand. "God puts people together for all sorts of reasons. I believe He does it so we can learn something we need from them. Everyone who comes into our lives is there for a specific reason, a season or perhaps a lifetime."

"I believe in that. When we learned Mom planned to marry Cobb, it made us stone crazy. That was a real difficult time for my brothers and me."

Fighting an urge to reach up and caress his smooth, handsome face, China smiled instead. "It obviously turned out okay. You all seem to get along so well."

"We do. After Zurich confronted Mom about her desire to marry Morgan, we found out he was nothing like our father. She told my brother that Morgan had kept food on our table and clothes on our backs when our alcoholic father regularly drank up his paycheck. Cobb also paid for our tuition and dorm fees at Buckley Academy."

China's starry gaze fell upon Zaire. "Buckley Academy! Now that's one prep school I've heard a lot of great things about." She thought back on what she'd witnessed with Bernice and Morgan. "They seem extremely good together. Is he accepted now?"

"We love and deeply respect Morgan. We've grown close to him. He's more than a father to us. He's a friend. The man treats Mom like the queen she is. Who can find fault with that? Speaking of reasons and seasons, what do you hope to learn from your experiences on the ranch? And has your seasonal or lifetime partner arrived yet?"

China's eyes suddenly grew moist. "My reason for being here is twofold. I came here to scatter my father's ashes over the land. He was a Texan and he loved this ranch. I've been going nonstop since my father died a few weeks ago. I am worn out and desperately need rest and relaxation. As for a lifetime partner, he's still out there wandering around somewhere."

"I'm sorry about your father. You have my deepest sympathy. If he loved this ranch, maybe I knew him. I've met most, if not all of our guests. What's his name?"

Sniffling, China wiped her nose with a napkin. "Brody Braxton."

In racking his brain, Zaire recognized the name but he couldn't put a face to it. Looking closely at China, he tried to see if she reminded him of anyone. "If it's not too hard on you, please tell me a little about your dad."

China's heart overflowed with sweet memories of her dad. "Brody was a wonderful father. He raised me alone, meeting my every need."

She cut it off there. No one needed to know her dark, personal despairs.

"He loved to horseback ride and he lived to conquer the ranch's mechanical bull. Unfortunately, he was dominated by it."

"Most men are. Now Mom and my aunts give that bucking mechanism pure hell. The ladies practice riding it a lot, timing each other to chart the length of time they stay on during each ride."

China roared with laughter. "I can actually imagine them riding the bull. They're a feisty bunch of women."

"Getting back to your dad, I believe I may've met him. Do you have a picture of him?"

China dug into her tote and pulled out her wallet. Flipping to the picture compartment, she came up with her favorite one of Brody by himself. "This is Dad," she said, handing the billfold to Zaire. "Does he look familiar?"

Zaire's eyes flared with instant recognition. "We've had a lot of interaction over the years. My brothers and I simply referred to him as Mr. B. He was an amazing storyteller, weaving some of the best yarns we've ever heard."

China was thrilled to know Zaire clearly remembered Brody.

"I remember Mr. B. so well. He loved to help out around here. You're right about his love for this place. He even talked about moving back to Texas after retirement to build a house on the several acres he owned. Are you selling his land?"

"I've thought of it but haven't made a final decision. I don't know what else I can do. I'm a city-loving girl from L.A. I can't begin to imagine Texas as my home."

"Life around here *is* a far cry from city living. I worked in the city for years but was constantly drawn back to my roots. I retired soon after I came up with a viable business plan to build on the vast acreage we own. I like peace and quiet. Our starry nights are unrivaled."

"I can see why you'd feel that way. Serenity *is* a perk of being way out here. I've never felt this kind of peace. What kind of work did you do before retiring?"

"Architectural engineering. I still do consulting work.

My education paid off when we drew up the plans to turn this place into an enormous entertainment venue. My work is my passion. I can barely wait to wake up to get my day started. At nightfall you can either find me around a campfire, involved in some activity with the guests or on my back patio stargazing. I easily lose myself to these surroundings."

China imagined Zaire seated in front of a campfire or relaxing on a patio. He obviously appreciated and preferred the simpler things in life. Ranching was his admitted passion. *What else was he ardent about?*

It was hard for China to picture him a loner. A sexy woman on his arm was an easier image to conjure up. He was masculine, steeped in virility. She had missed an opportunity to inquire about his possible partner when he'd boldly asked about hers. It wasn't like her to let too many things get by, but Zaire kept her in a tizzy.

The urge to reach over and squeeze one of Zaire's rock-hard thighs had China edgy. She wanted to stay with him— and she also wanted to run away from his strong presence, all at the same time. China needed to will her mind to blankness. Zaire occupied way too much room inside her head.

Zaire looked at his watch. "It's time to get back. I have a riding lesson."

"I know. I signed up for the riding session to conquer my fear of horses. Getting on one is the only way I can do it," China confessed.

Zaire's eyes filled with admiration. "When something scares us, finding a way to deal with it is smart. I promise to make your first riding experience a good one."

China grinned. "Thank you. And I promise to hold you to your promise."

* * *

Getting China up on a horse wouldn't be anywhere as easy as Zaire had initially thought. Each time she backed away from Ebony Dancer, she put more and more space between her and the jet-black filly. The other students had already mounted—and she was holding up the class.

Zaire took China aside. "In the interest of time, I have to start the class. There's an hour and a half break between this riding session and my calf-roping event. Let me work with the others, then give you a private lesson. Okay?"

Though relieved by his gracious suggestion, China looked embarrassed. "I'll stay and watch. Maybe it'll help get my nerve up."

He pointed at the white fence. "Stand on the other side or sit on it. Just be careful. Don't want you to fall off and get hurt."

Giving Zaire a thumbs-up, China scurried from the corralling ring and propped herself comfortably on the pristine fence posts. Watching the lesson was better than tackling it, especially while fear still ran rampant through her.

Several minutes into the lesson, China recognized Zaire as a master at his work. The first thing he'd accomplished was gaining the riders' trust in his abilities to instruct. Thoroughly explaining each step he'd take them through, his tone was steady, calming.

Children didn't look the least bit scared, making China feel rather silly. She looked forward to the private lesson and hoped Zaire didn't think it was a contrived plan to get him alone. As she thought more about it, she easily concluded being alone with him wasn't such a bad idea.

Walking over to the fence, Zaire helped China down. "Now you can have my undivided attention. Here's what we're going to do. I think you should ride with me before you attempt to get on a horse alone. We'll move along at a slow pace."

Picturing herself on the same horse with Zaire, China's heart leapt. "I love your idea." Then her smile turned to a frown. "But I'm still scared."

"Wait here. Be right back. It'll be okay," he said, his tone soothing, promising. He and two ranch hands led the horses inside a gray metal barn right behind the corral.

Seated atop Thunder, galloping at a steady pace, Zaire rode back to China and rapidly dismounted. "I need you to trust me, China. Can you do that?"

Literally shaking in her boots, China nodded. "I'll try."

Taking her by the hand, he led her over to Thunder. "Stay, boy," he commanded calmly. Taking a minute to think about whether to put her on the horse or get on first and help her up afterward, he decided on the latter. Remounting, he reached down a hand to her. Fear still written in her eyes, she reluctantly joined her hand with his.

In the next instant, Zaire had China seated in front of him. Putting her on the back of the horse couldn't guarantee her safety, so he thought it best to guide from the rear. She was a little thing. Her size left him plenty of room to maneuver.

China felt exhilarated with Zaire seated right behind her. It was hot and muggy, but being on fire for him had her even hotter. Without thinking of consequences, she laid her head back against his chest. The wind tousled her hair from behind and above. China didn't care what she looked like, not while she felt such peace.

This was not the China Braxton she was used to. Usually every strand of her hair had to be in place, and her clothes had to be immaculate and wrinkle-free or she'd feel disheveled and frumpy. She already understood why her father had loved the ranch. Out here in the open spaces, she felt her mountain of burdens rapidly rolling away.

Trotting Thunder slowly around the ring, talking to China at the same time, Zaire actually felt her beginning to relax. He snapped the reins, causing Thunder to pick up speed. "Lean forward and whisper near his ear. Gently stroke his neck and mane," he instructed. "Thunder loves to be stroked, especially by a beautiful woman."

Zaire's pointed statement had China cringing, though she knew it shouldn't.

Why had he made a point to say that beautiful women stroked Thunder?

So, maybe she had her answer. Zaire as a loner had been a half-baked thought.

Friendship was probably all they could ever have.

"Mom and my aunts have spoiled Thunder rotten. Every time they come to the stables, they visit his stall and bring him apples and carrots. He gets plenty of pampering from those beautiful ladies and from some of our female guests."

"What about your girlfriends? Do they spoil him, too?" Unable to believe she'd asked him that, she bit down on her tongue as a punishment for her rudeness.

"Girlfriends! That's a nice thought to wrap my head around, but I don't have any. Nor do I have *a* girlfriend. It's hard to get to know women when you're a workaholic. My father was an alcoholic, and this son of his is obsessed with working hard."

"I'm sorry, Zaire. I shouldn't have stuck my nose in your private business."

"Don't worry about it." Zaire laughed inwardly.

Zaire was surprised he was opening up to China in such a personal way. It wasn't like him to share his deepest feelings, especially the painful ones. His real troubles with women started when he moved to the ranch. Most women didn't share his enthusiasm for his cowboy lifestyle, though a few pretended to.

If only she knew how much I've let her in. Why is she so easy for me to spill my guts to? Look at her pretty face and those liquid chocolate eyes. Now, pal, ask yourself the same question again.

Zaire sighed. Opening up to China was easy because she had listened closely to him and seemed to care about what he had to say. He liked talking to her.

Admit it, man. You're lonely as hell, and she turns you on. She's also the only woman who has even come close to sparking your interest.

Now that China seemed comfortable straddling Thunder, Zaire guided the horse out of the corral and onto the open range. Maybe once she felt the wind at her face and breathed in the clean air, she'd come to love it here as much as he did. Not even his brothers knew every square inch of the ranch like he did. There were so many exciting wonders to see.

Thinking about the big oak tree he loved to sit under during his downtime, Zaire steered Thunder in its direction. Never had he shared his private haunts with a woman, but he wanted China to see and feel every special spot there was.

Zaire knew she'd be gone from his life all too soon. If he didn't make the most of the time China was within his reach, she'd never know why he loved the ranch so much. It was a dangerously high hope, but maybe, just maybe, she'd also fall in love with Whispering Lakes Ranch.

Perhaps China can fall in love with me, too.

* * *

After helping China dismount, Zaire removed a bedroll and a couple of bottles of water from twin saddlebags. One bag was insulated for hot and cold. Unfurling the bedroll, he spread it out under the tree. Time was short. He thought of calling the ranch to have Zane take over his roping event, but he immediately thought better of it. The fear of losing his mind over a woman who'd soon leave the ranch held him back.

Sipping on an ice-cold bottle of water, China carefully studied the sturdy oak. "It's a beautiful tree and looks like a very old one."

"It is old. Go ahead and stretch out and relax. It'll welcome your presence."

"I think I will. It looks inviting." China looked into his eyes. "By the way, I loved the ride out here. It was much smoother than I anticipated. You stole my fear right out from under me."

Zaire nodded. "That's all well and good, but you still have to learn to ride solo. Only then will you rid yourself of the phobia permanently."

China sat down and instantly took off her footwear, wiggling her toes to celebrate the freedom. "I like how tranquil my spirit feels."

The pillow Zaire had placed on the bedroll drew China's head down to it like a magnet to metal. She looked up at the tree. "The branches are so full that they're completely sheltering me from the sun's blazing heat." Within a matter of seconds, China's eyes involuntarily drooped.

Sitting down on a navy wool blanket he'd laid out next to the bedroll, Zaire had a desire to run his fingers through China's hair. Thoughts of kissing her juicy lips came next.

Quickly, he decided it was a bad move on his part. China would have to offer him her sweet mouth. He wasn't into taking anything not given freely.

By the time Zaire thought of the walkie-talkie he always carried, an hour and a half had passed. It was near time to leave. He hated to awaken China, who looked so peaceful. Indulging in the unthinkable, the very thing he'd decided against a short while ago, he got up and retrieved the walkie-talkie.

Punching in a three digit code, Zaire waited for a response. "Zane, I need a favor." He went on to tell his brother why he was calling.

"Not a problem, bro. I got your back."

Fortunately the Kingdom family worked as a harmonious unit. Zane hadn't hesitated in agreeing to take over the event. Knowing his scheduled roping class was in capable hands, Zaire returned to his seat. Removing his cowboy boots, he laid his head close to China's, keeping enough distance not to accidentally disturb her.

Minutes later, Zaire joined China in a late-afternoon nap.

Chapter 3

Several hours later, China awakened to find Zaire asleep. Her heart grew full at the sight of such a gorgeous man. She'd love to watch him slumber like a newborn for hours, but she was concerned over his next class.

Shaking him ever so gently, China whispered softly, "Zaire, Zaire, wake up."

Peering up at China, a charming smile formed on Zaire's luscious lips. "Looks like we both fell asleep. You okay, China Doll?"

China Doll! She smiled.

"I'm fine. But I woke you 'cause of your next event. I've got a sinking feeling you've missed it." She pulled on her boots. "We've been here awhile."

No one had ever called her China Doll. It was too sweet for mere words. However, the expression in her eyes probably revealed to him the joy she felt.

Zaire smiled, reading her expression perfectly. "I knew I missed it."

"You knew?" China appeared genuinely surprised.

Zaire sat upright. Following China's lead, he put his boots back on. "It's covered. I didn't want to wake you so I called Zane to take over for me. I'm sure the family is in shock. That is, if Zane has already told them. Knowing him, I'm sure he did…in his usual melodramatic way."

China frowned. "Why would it shock them?"

"Unless something extremely important comes up, I rarely ask anyone to take over a duty for me. I never outright shirk duties or responsibilities. I'm sure they're all dying to know the reason why I didn't make it back in time. My family can be a pretty gossipy circle."

Did it have anything to do with her? China wondered. Smiling broadly, she sure hoped so. "Sorry if I caused trouble for you, Zaire."

"You didn't. It was my decision to stay. I wanted to be here. You were sleeping peacefully and I was tired so I decided to lie down and regroup. Zane, Zurich and Morgan can cover all events and classes. Trust me, no harm was done."

"I'm glad." Picking up her tote, China reached in and removed her hairbrush.

"Fixing your hair will be for nothing. The wind blows up a storm this time of day." Picking up his Stetson, he settled it onto her head. "This should help some. To make you an official cowgirl, we'll have to get you your own. The ones in our gift shop are top quality."

Slipping down over China's eyes, the hat nearly swallowed up her head. It was way too big, but she wouldn't think of taking it off. That he'd given it up to her made her feel special.

Wishing she could preserve the blissful serenity encircling her, China stretched her arms up high.

As the couple walked toward Thunder, tethered to a sturdy tree branch and eating grass and leaves, Zaire wished he could take hold of China's hand. He wanted to somehow convey his interest in getting better acquainted with her, but he was new at making his feelings known. He hadn't had a date in ages, shying away from females by design. China made him feel differently, but he was still leery.

Zaire settled down Thunder and walked China to her car. Her ride with him had built some confidence and made her less intimidated by horses.

Zaire stopped in front of her car. "Well, it looks like this is it for now. Think you'll make it to the club this evening? A different band is featured tonight."

China nodded. "I'd already decided to drop in. I also plan to eat dinner in the main dining room. I hear you all cook up the fish caught on the trip. I can't wait to taste the fruits of my labor." She laughed. "And your labor, too, of course. I couldn't have landed those beauties if you hadn't helped."

While trying to decide if he should let a perfect opportunity like this pass him by, Zaire's heart hammered away. A desire to share a table with her over dinner was strong. "I'd like us to have dinner together. That is, if you don't have other plans."

China's smile was effervescent. "What's so wonderful about this moment was my desire to ask you the same thing. Is seven-thirty good?"

Glad he'd taken the risk, Zaire felt relieved. "The time is fine. I'll reserve us a table. Mom and Morgan do the cooking. Rest assured you'll be served a fish dinner from the babies you nabbed."

"How can anyone know what fish belongs to whom?" China inquired.

"We give out colored clips to guests before the trip. I didn't give you any because it looked as if you'd be with Zane's group. I had a few extra ones in my pocket so I used them on yours after we hauled them aboard. I later told Mom you had orange. We try to make sure everyone gets some of what they reeled in, but it's not always possible. Lots of folks don't catch a thing, but there's always enough fish to go around."

"That *is* really special." Standing on tiptoes, China kissed Zaire on the cheek. "Thanks for a beautiful day! I enjoyed it. See you at dinner."

Zaire started to offer to pick up China at her cabin, but then thought it might be too much. One step at a time, he told himself. Slow and easy beats fast and hard.

While stepping out of the shower, China suddenly felt light-headed. Slowly she made her way to the bed. Pulling back the comforter, she climbed in, propping her feet on two pillows. Reaching over to retrieve the nightstand clock, she set the alarm, giving herself plenty of time to dress and make it to the dining room.

After tossing and turning for nearly a half hour, China feared sleep would elude her. It hadn't been too long ago that she and Zaire had awakened under the oak tree. With her thoughts turning to the man who caused her heart to flip-flop, dance, sing and turn somersaults, she smiled.

China's age-old fears about love quickly gripped her heart.

Her previous romantic relationships hadn't worked because she hadn't been able to stop comparing herself to her mother. Thoughts of one day running off and leaving her family behind haunted her constantly. The possibility of repeating such a destructive offense made her cringe every time she dared to think about her mother leaving her dad.

Brody had tried to tell China she wasn't her mother and that she had to stop believing she'd do the same type of things. Desertion wasn't hereditary. Brody didn't blame Camille for leaving them. He actually thought it took a lot of guts to take responsibility for one's own happiness. According to his wife, she hadn't been happy for years.

The letter her mother had left behind said it hadn't taken her long to learn she wasn't cut out to be a wife or mother, citing selfishness for the reason she'd left her family. Brody wasn't to blame for anything Camille had felt or had written in the letter. Camille suffered from clinical depression. He'd gone to his death never knowing that, at 16, his daughter had read the letter Camille had written to her husband.

Camille had loved both her husband and daughter. She had simply yearned for freedom.

China had only recently stopped blaming her mother for her painful childhood. Brody had constantly instilled in her that she was solely responsible for her own happiness. It would've broken his heart to know his only child had learned that her birth had made her mother's life even more unbearable.

The yearly birthday and Christmas cards China received from Camille were as close as she'd ever been to her mother since her departure. China had often wished Camille would one day drop back into her life but refused to set herself up for another major letdown.

China had learned to accept things for what they were. She wasn't bitter or angry anymore. She truly loved her mother, regardless of why she'd left. The last thing she wanted was to have her mother go away like Brody had. His departure was final.

Stepping into the dimly lit dining room, China looked around for Zaire. She'd hoped he would've been waiting outside for her. Standing at the front entry for several minutes proved futile. Appearing cool and collected, she wore a cute capped-sleeve sheath in bright red, perfectly paired with fashionable red-and-white sandals.

Coming up behind China, Bernice gently tapped her on the shoulder.

A bright smile already in place, China turned. "Hi, Ms. Bernice, how are you?"

"I'm well, young lady. How *has* your day been?"

China sensed an underlying meaning in Bernice's remark by the way she'd voiced it. "I loved every moment of it. Zaire is a perfect instructor and tour guide."

Bernice beamed with pride. "That boy of mine *is* wonderful. He called me to tell you he's running a little late." She pointed at a cozy corner spot. "That's the table he reserved. Want to come into the kitchen with me before you get settled?"

"I'd like that." China smiled brightly. "How was frying up all that fish?"

"Cooking is second nature to me, child. Some of our guests like fish broiled or mesquite grilled so we do our best to prepare it to order. Most folks enjoy it fried. You had quite a catch. More fish than I've seen one person catch in a while."

Heading toward the double doors in the rear, China walked alongside Bernice. "I'm proud of my haul. Zaire helped out big-time. My dad would've been thrilled."

"Zaire mentioned your dad to me. Our family is very fa-

miliar with Mr. B. He was a special man. He and Morgan
loved to play poker. Both men had an insatiable desire to
master our mechanical bull." Bernice laughed. "Morgan
and Brody called it Mr. Red. Let's just say they had fun
being thrown off and then scrambling to get right back on."

"I've heard so much about the bull from Dad. He talked
about Mr. Red a lot."

"Think you'll try riding old Red, China?"

China nodded. "With Dad looking down on me, I know
he'd be disappointed if I didn't give it a whirl. Is Mr. Red
really so tough to ride?"

"For some folks he is." Opening the double doors by
hitting a metal button, Bernice let China precede her. "It
depends a lot on the bull's settings. Most men try riding it
on the highest one. It's a macho thing. Many guys fail for
that reason alone."

China chuckled. "I hear you and your sisters are pretty
good at riding it."

"Practice makes perfect in some instances, but we're
far from it. We've earned quite a bit of envy around here.
After mastering each setting, we keep breaking our own
timing records. Josephine is the best. She stays on longer
than anyone."

China cracked up. "I can't wait to try it out. You make
it sound exciting."

"It *is* exciting, but the kitchen is my favorite hangout. We
purchased all brand-new appliances for this one last year."
Bernice spread her arms wide. "I love stainless steel. It's
easy to clean." Bernice enjoyed showing China around her
favorite haunt, obviously proud of the state-of-the-art cooking gallery. She introduced China to their chefs and other
kitchen staff, something she rarely did. Bernice felt really
good about China.

Bernice peered at the large clock. "I'd better get you

to your table. If Zaire hasn't made it yet, he'll be here any minute. There's no way he'd miss out on this evening. He's looking forward to it."

China wanted to probe further into Bernice's comments, but she didn't dare.

Was Zaire really looking forward to spending more time with her?

Zaire entered the kitchen at the same time Bernice and China exited. Wasting no time, he pulled his mother into his arms. Turning to face China, his eyes danced with pleasure as he checked her out from head to toe. That she looked well-rested pleased him. The withered look she'd worn earlier had worried him.

Zaire's eyes then connected with his mother's hopeful gaze. The look he gave her back let her know he was entertaining optimism, surprisingly so.

Smiling, he extended his arm to China. "Our table's ready for us, Miss Lady."

China giggled, hating her immature response. She'd noticed the interesting look he'd given his mother. Bernice had lifted her eyebrows over what she'd interpreted the glance to mean. China couldn't help wondering what each expression meant.

A single yellow rose nesting in a crystal bud vase put a lovely smile on China's lips. Looking around with practiced discretion, she saw that the other centerpieces were pillar candles inside glass holders. The rose was specifically intended for her.

Lifting the vase, China inhaled the delicate scent of the rose. "Mm, I love most flowers, but roses are my favorite. Thank you."

"You're welcome!" He pulled out her chair. "Ready to taste the fish you caught?"

"I can hardly wait." China sat down and placed the linen napkin on her lap. "I enjoyed touring the fabulous kitchen. It's a very busy place."

"Newly remodeled and busy nearly twenty-four hours a day. If you ever come back, you'll notice more wear and tear. Mom is magical at cleaning, but the shine does go away."

"I would think so. Are your aunts coming in for dinner?"

Glancing at his watch, Zaire laughed. "They're probably at bingo already. Our favorite ladies play bingo in town every Saturday evening. They want to make it a part of our activities schedule, but I don't want to incorporate gambling here. It doesn't work for me. Zurich and Zane side with me on the issue."

China raised an eyebrow. "Do you really consider bingo gambling?"

"If money is involved, it's gambling. We have to think about the kids. If our aunts wanted to conduct bingo games using prizes instead of money, I'd be okay with it."

Appearing suddenly at the table, Gayle interrupted the couple's conversation, greeting China with a melodic hello and a sweet smile. She then kissed the top of Zaire's head. "I'm only filling in for a half hour or so. One of the waitresses is sick. What do you two want for sides? We have coleslaw, potato and macaroni salads, French fries and onion rings."

China smiled. "I'd like macaroni salad."

"Come on now, Gayle. You've been around our family enough to know I like potato salad with fish," Zaire playfully scolded.

Gayle laughed. "You could've had a change in taste. Macaroni and potato salad are coming right up."

"There you go," he teased, laughing.

Gayle pulled a face. "I'll be back with your meals."

"Of the two salads, which is your favorite?" China asked Zaire.

"I love them both, but I always eat potato salad with fish. If Mom fixes deviled eggs while you're here, line up in a hurry."

"Deviled eggs are spring and summer treats at our house. Dad was a superb chef. I was allowed to choose my foods and saw it as a blessing, since all parents aren't able to give their children choices. Never did I have to eat anything I didn't like, but I was encouraged to at least taste a variety of foods."

"You haven't mentioned your mom yet. Did she cook for you, too?"

China sucked in a calming breath. "I don't know my mother. Let me rephrase that. I didn't grow up with my mother, but I knew her as much as any four-year-old is capable of. Memories fade."

"I won't pry," Zaire said with understanding. "If you ever want to talk about your mother, I'm a great listener."

China shuddered. "Let me get it out and over with. Suffering from clinical depression, Mom believed having a baby would solve her problems. It only ended up making matters worse. To hopefully make a new start, Mom left."

Zaire's curiosity was heightened. "Are you two in contact now?"

"She sends me birthday and Christmas cards every year. Camille Braxton lives in Atlanta. I haven't seen her since the day she left, a day I don't even remember. She's still using Dad's surname so I'm assuming she didn't remarry."

"Would you welcome her back into your life if she reappeared?"

"I'd love to see her and sit down for a chat. Believe it or not, I have no desire to make her pay for anything. My father believes she's been harder on herself than anyone.

Dad forgave her and I've come to terms with it. I still miss having my family around, even though I've dealt with my lonely childhood."

Gayle was back, and it was perfect timing, in Zaire's opinion. The conversation had gotten pretty weighty. China had held up well, but he didn't want her to relive what probably hurt her more than she'd admit. He knew the cross she bore was heavy.

Zaire's life had also been severely damaged at the hands of a parent. It had taken the Kingdom brothers a long time to forgive Macon, who had come back into Bernice's life when he was ill and dying. Despite loudly voiced opposition from her sons and sisters, Bernice had taken Macon into her home, where she'd nursed her estranged husband's fragile body until the day of his demise.

A half hour later, China and Zaire pushed back from the table. The bass and catfish were delicious, light and flaky. For dessert China had chosen only one scoop of lime sherbet, since her stomach was nearly full.

"You want anything else, China?"

China caressed her stomach. "Nothing more will fit in here. No, thanks. I'm full and satisfied."

"I'm glad you enjoyed your meal."

Gayle came back to the table. Pausing for a moment, she looked from Zaire to China. "Tomorrow is Sunday. Guests have lots of leisure time. We're having an evening baby shower for Hailey. We'd love for you to join us, China. You'll have a good time."

Zaire was willing to bet that inviting China to the shower was his mother's idea. Single women just didn't come to the ranch alone, and Bernice had mentioned to her family she planned to include China in their activities. After learning

China was Mr. B.'s daughter, Bernice felt even stronger about looking after her. She had always wanted a daughter.

"Thank you. I'll come, but I need a gift."

Gayle smiled. "I can pick up something for you. I'm going into town early in the morning. Let me know your price range."

"I'll tell you what. I'll go back and get some cash before the band starts so you won't have to spend your money."

"Not necessary. We'll square it at some point. See you guys at the club. The band playing tonight is hot. Southern Fever has an amazing female vocalist."

"I love the name." China used her hand to fan herself in a playful way. "The band sounds hot."

China thought the band was living up to their name. The five guys and one woman indulged their audience in a variety of music genres. From R&B to Country-Western, they'd performed each sound like true professionals. Zaire loved the blues and earlier confessed to China that he also had it bad for Country-Western.

"Would you like to dance, China?"

"Since I haven't been able to keep still, I think it's a good idea."

Zaire chuckled. "I noticed."

Zaire extended his hand to China. Walking toward the dance floor, his arm fell loosely about her waist.

Zaire's tender hand on her waist had China's body heating up from within. His touch was innocent yet it produced fiery sensations. She had a hard time keeping her mind from wandering into dangerous territory. Images of his hands hotly roving intimate places on her body danced in her head.

Concentrating on the music helped China take her mind off Zaire seducing her. While dancing, she noticed how light he was on his feet. The sexy gyrations of his hips sent her mind wandering once again.

A slow song came on, and Zaire brought China closer to him in one fluid motion.

Looking up at him, China smiled. "The band is fantastic. Love their style."

"Our other guests love their brand of entertainment. They're here at least one weekend a month. I'd bring them in more often if it was up to me. But they're in high demand around these parts. They play clubs all over Brownsville and at posh resorts on South Padre Island. They *are* touted as the very best."

While making their way back to the table, China spotted Gayle and Zane headed toward them. "There's your brother and Gayle."

He looked at his watch. "It's nearly ten. My aunts will appear any minute. Bingo was over at nine. They love Southern Fever more than any band that's played here."

China nodded. "I bet they do." Laughing, she reclaimed her chair. "Do your aunts go out on dates?"

Zaire's eyes widened. "Do they ever? My aunts have been widowed for years. They're the center of attention for many elderly gentlemen around here. My aunts started a senior center on the property. Female members outnumber the males, but everyone has a great time together. They're like one big happy family. I don't think a week goes by that one of my aunts doesn't receive a marriage proposal."

China was amused. "I see why. They're a healthy, lively crew."

Taking seats on the other side of the table, Gayle and Zane greeted Zaire and China. The couples began conversing, raising their voices to be heard over the band.

They talked about everything from current events to

some of the more interesting guests at the ranch, like Mrs. Cotton.

Covertly observing Zane and Gayle, China wondered how long the couple had been together. Their hands touched and eyes locked constantly. He held on to her every word, just as she did his. A special aura surrounded them, as if they were everything to one another.

Gayle placed her folded hands on the table. "China, I bet you love living in Los Angeles. I've always wanted to go there."

China rolled her eyes. "It's an unbelievable place to live. Everything you've read about it is true. There's always something exciting to do in L.A. You don't ever have to be bored."

Zane grinned. "It doesn't get boring around here either, but we do live a totally different lifestyle than folks in California."

Glad his brother's remarks weren't sarcastic, Zaire sighed with relief. Before Gayle had come into Zane's life, he had been a known player.

China couldn't read the expression in Zaire's eyes. He had told her that Zurich was totally committed to Hailey, loving her more than anything in the world, but he hadn't said much about Zane and Gayle.

Would Zaire be just as committed to someone special in his life as his older brother?

After looking up at the brilliant stars, China turned her attention back to Zaire. "I can't believe it's already two o'clock Sunday morning. Time just flew by. Thanks for walking me to my car. Maybe I'll see you around tomorrow."

Zaire wanted to ask China if he could follow her home, but he knew it was late and he shouldn't intrude upon her private space. He had to keep reminding himself that she was a guest. She wasn't at his disposal nor was she there for his pleasure.

As Zaire leaned in to kiss her cheek, China suddenly fainted, slumping forward and sliding down his body. Getting a tight hold on her, he kept her from hitting the ground. China's eyes rolled back and only the whites were exposed. Zaire was gravely concerned. "China," he called out anxiously.

Unable to hold her up and open the car door at the same time, he wasn't sure what to do. Taking her back inside the club was a thought he quickly dismissed. He didn't want everyone gawking and wondering if she was drunk.

Only seconds after Zaire had said a silent prayer, Zane and Gayle came outside.

"Zane," Zaire yelled, "I need help over here. Please hurry."

Zane and Gayle rushed over to China's car. "What's going on?" Zane asked.

"I need you to help me get her to the E.R.," Zaire shouted.

"Sure. Let me get the truck. Gayle, stay here with them. I'll be right back."

No sooner had Zane taken off running than China slowly came to. Her eyes, wide with fear, glazed over like ice. A few seconds later, she was able to bring things into focus. "What happened to me? I feel weird. My head is killing me."

"You fainted. It'll be okay," Zaire soothed, gently stroking her back. "Zane is getting the truck to take you to a Brownsville E.R."

China gingerly shook her head. "No, please, I don't want to go to a hospital. Can you just get me back to my room? I'll be fine once I lie down and rest."

Zaire looked to Gayle for an answer.

Appearing worried, all Gayle could do was shrug.

Zaire was concerned. "Okay, China. Where are your keys?"

"Inside my purse," China responded.

He didn't like how breathless she sounded. "Gayle, see if you can locate her car keys." Zaire remained calm despite his deep concern for China's well-being.

Gayle rummaged through China's purse until she came up with a key chain. Before locating the car key, she saw the cabin key.

The car alarm sounded when Gayle opened the door, scaring the daylights out of her. Quelling the senseless fear, she quickly pressed the button to turn it off. Running around the car, she opened the driver's door. "Do you want us to follow you to the cabin? I can drive your SUV. Zane can trail us in his truck."

"Please. She'll need you to help her get undressed and into bed."

Gayle frowned. "Are you sure we shouldn't get her to the E.R.?"

"No," China said, struggling to hold up her head. "This happened because I'm totally worn out. I'll be fine after I get some sleep. Fatigue is my biggest adversary."

Zaire sided with Gayle's recommendations, but he had to respect China's wishes. He lifted China and carried her around to the passenger side. Practicing extreme caution, Zaire settled her onto the leather seat and secured the seat belt.

Pulling his truck up beside China's car, Zane jumped out. "How's she doing now?" Worry creased his brow. "Is she any better?"

China's hand wave was as weak as she looked. "I'm

okay, Zane. Just need to get to bed and rest. I need to slow down the frantic pace."

China's eyes suddenly closed again. Zaire sent up a quiet supplication, praying he was doing the right thing by her. "Let's get her back to her cabin."

Pacing the grounds in front of cabin nine, Zaire was worried and impatient.

Waiting on Gayle to come out and update him on China's condition had him feeling insane. Talking quietly with Zane, he told him what had happened just before China's world had shorted out like a blown lightbulb. Zaire was now emotional.

Just when Zaire thought he couldn't deal with not knowing for another second, the cabin door opened. With the crook of her forefinger, Gayle summoned the two men to come back inside. She took Zaire by the hand. "She's doing okay. I think I've convinced her to see a doctor."

"I'm grateful for that. This is unsettling," Zaire told Gayle. "I've already called Dr. Jenkins. He's coming by as soon as he can."

Harold Jenkins had been the Kingdom family doctor for many years. In hopes of making life easier for Bernice, the lifelong family friend and general practitioner had taken it upon himself to make house calls to treat a sickly Macon. In turn, the Kingdoms sent numerous patient referrals his way. If a guest had to seek medical treatment, his business card was handed out, and one was also put inside the resort's information packets.

"China might like your idea a lot better. She's adamant about not going to an E.R.," Gayle remarked. "She *is* a nurse."

Zane took Gayle by the hand, then made eye contact

with his brother. "We'll leave it up to you to tell China your game plan, Zaire. We're out of here, bro."

"Thanks, guys. I'm glad you were around to help. I couldn't have done this alone." Zaire walked Zane and Gayle to the truck. "See you later."

Zaire stood stock-still until he heard Zane's truck roar to life. This was an awkward position for him to be in. He'd never taken on a role like this before. Looking after China seemed the most natural thing in the world to do, but it wasn't. As soon as he stepped inside, he looked over at the bedroom entry. Behind the closed door lay an intriguing woman he was attracted to on so many levels. *A city girl.* Dismissing his thoughts, Zaire went to the door and knocked.

"Come on in," China called out, her voice weak and weary.

Zaire's breath caught at the sight of China looking pale and vulnerable, yet so angelic. He hadn't prepared himself for this strong reaction to her. The top of her white silk gown had him wondering what she wore under it. He actually envied the material caressing her body. The flowing silk was closer to her than he'd probably ever get.

China looked over at the recliner. "Please have a seat."

Feeling like he had no will of his own, Zaire sat. "How're you feeling?"

China sighed deeply. "I have a painful headache. Sorry I ruined your evening."

Zaire waved off her concerns. "You did no such thing. Besides, the club was closing. What do you think happened to you back there?"

"Exhaustion," China confessed. "Ever since Dad died I've pushed myself hard. If I stopped going, I feared I'd fall apart emotionally. I couldn't sleep, couldn't rest. I didn't want to go to bed just to lie awake and rehash the beautiful memories." Tears sprang to her eyes. "Have you ever missed someone to the point of not believing you'd survive another minute without them? That's how much I miss Dad."

China's gut-wrenching cries had Zaire out of his seat, pulling her into his arms. "I won't tell you not to cry. You need to feel the pain. Crying is soul cleansing."

Choking up even more, China sobbed hard. "I don't... want...to cry."

"Then you won't begin to deal with the hurt. You'll never forget your dad or the wonderful times you spent together. Don't deny yourself the company of those great memories. They represent so much of your life. Not everyone gets to experience the love you and Mr. B. had."

Mindlessly stroking her hair, Zaire felt responsible for calming her down. The last time he was faced with a grieving woman was when his mother had laid their father to rest. Bernice had been inconsolable that day. Despite all the abuse she'd taken from her husband and the father of her three sons, her sorrow had been unyielding.

Zaire tenderly laid China's head back against the pillow. He wanted to kiss her until she was oblivious to the pain, but he put some distance between them, hoping it would keep him honest. This wasn't the time to make any kind of intimate move on her. A real man never took advantage of a woman in any moment of weakness. He prided himself on the strength of his integrity. Although he hadn't been with a woman in a long time, he hadn't forgotten how to treat one well.

China was worthy of royal treatment. Zaire believed it with his whole heart.

Chapter 4

Zaire lifted his body from the mattress long enough to pull the comforter up under China's chin. Her bare arms tantalized him and the low-cut bodice of her gown showed the mesmerizing swells of perky breasts. The alluring vision had already gotten to him. His manhood had been on the warpath from the moment he'd first taken her back into his arms. It was hard to be immune to someone who was in such a helpless state.

"I was worried about you, China. I called our family doctor. He'll be out here any minute. Harold Jenkins is a fantastic doctor. I think you'll like him."

Frowning, China sighed. "I don't need a doctor, just more rest. I won't get up as early for the next couple of days or so. This *is* vacation time."

Skeptical, Zaire raised an eyebrow. "Rest may do it, but I'd be more comfortable if you'd let Dr. Jenkins check you out."

China shook her head in the negative. "I already know what he'll tell me. I'm a nurse, remember?"

"Of course I remember, but you're not a doctor," Zaire replied. "I don't want you to stay here while you're sick. I'm willing to give you a full refund. Or I can offer you a rain check to come back when you're feeling better?"

China pursed her lips. "Afraid I'll sue you?"

Zaire shot her a scolding glance. "Sue me for what?"

"I did faint. If something happens to me on the ranch, maybe you think I'd hold you liable. If you hadn't been there to catch me, I could've hit the ground and suffered a head injury."

Zaire saw this as a no-win situation. China had a stubborn, determined look in her eyes. He was worried…but not about any lawsuit. His ranch was insured to cover all guests against accidents or unexpected illnesses.

Conveying his feelings to her was a huge problem for him, especially when she wasn't in a mood to listen. It was obvious she didn't want to hear his sensible arguments. Zaire knew four other ladies just as stubborn as this one. He had yet to reign victorious in any battle his mother and aunts had been determined to win.

China swatted away the moisture from her eyes. "Missing Dad is a constant longing, a terminal aching." She began sobbing anew.

Despite China's stubbornness, Zaire sympathized with her obvious distress. "Death is always a hard pill to swallow. I know it for a fact."

Zaire recalled how he and his brothers had bawled on the day of Macon's funeral. They still cried over his memory, but now the tears were bittersweet. Knowing Macon could no longer hurt his family was the sweet part. The bitterness was for what they'd wanted so desperately from Macon and hadn't gotten.

Macon hadn't been able to teach his sons strong leadership skills, which they'd obtained through leadership classes at a military prep school, Buckley Academy. Zaire had also attended leadership seminars while working at an engineering company. Zurich was a retired Air Force officer and commander and had been required to attend leadership programs throughout his military career. As a teacher, Zane was groomed in leadership.

The sons hadn't been loved unconditionally by Macon. Showing pride in his boys was an impossible task for a man ruled by alcohol. Mean as a snake, he had constantly spewed poisonous venom at his family.

Zaire got to his feet. "I should go. I'll make sure you're checked on a little later. Is there anything I can get you before I leave?"

China shook her head. "Everything is fine. Sleep will help replenish my energy." Suddenly grabbing both sides of her head, she moaned. "Migraine," she complained.

Zaire rushed back to her side. Taking her into his arms again, he slowly rocked her back and forth. "Do you feel faint?"

"No but the throbbing pain is intense." Her eyes widened. "No more rocking, please. The motion is nauseating. Can you please bring a wastebasket closer to the bed and get my migraine prescription from the bathroom cabinet?"

After easing China's head back onto a pillow, Zaire grabbed a plastic-lined wastebasket and set it right next to the bed. Hurrying into the bathroom, he grabbed a box of tissues and the prescription. Carrying the items back to the bedroom, he placed them on the nightstand. "Can I do anything else?"

A blank stare in China's eyes scared Zaire. As her eyelids drooped, his heart pounded hard again. *Had she passed out or merely fallen asleep?*

The rise and fall of China's chest appeared normal and her breathing was even. Slowly backing up until he reached the recliner, he dropped down onto it. Resigning himself to keeping an eye on her wasn't a hard decision.

Zaire didn't think China should be left alone, not when she'd complained of a painful headache and nausea. He'd like nothing better than to lie in bed with her, but lying next to her would be his undoing.

China awakened an hour and forty-five minutes later and found Zaire asleep in the recliner. His presence surprised her. As she gave it more thought, she determined it wasn't so surprising. He was a sensitive, caring man.

Lifting her head from the pillow, China slowly lowered it. Her head felt better. The migraine medication had done its job. The tablets her doctor had prescribed for her right after her father's demise, when she'd gotten the first headaches, were close at hand.

Looking around the room, China didn't see any of her personal items. The closet door was standing open and empty. Her clothes were gone. How had they vanished without her knowledge? Then she saw her suitcases standing upright in the corner. Realizing he'd packed up her things to ship her off his ranch was a defeating, crashing blow to her ego and her heart.

Glaring darkly at a sleeping Zaire, China slowly sat up again. This time she carefully swung her legs to the side of the mattress. Slipping cautiously out of bed, she made her way to the luggage. Opening the larger bag first, she dumped its contents. From the smaller bag, she retrieved her makeup kit to put back in the bathroom.

After hanging her clothes back in the closet, she returned her intimate apparel to the dresser drawers. Once she'd filled a glass with water, she went back to bed. Shaking a pill from the prescription bottle, China gulped it down and pulled the comforter up over her. Putting her things away had taken nearly all of her strength. Zaire hadn't moved an inch.

Zaire awakened shortly after China had gone back to bed. Looking over at her, he smiled brightly. "Feeling better?"

China fought the wild urge to go off on Zaire. *Who in the hell did he think he was to try and send her packing?* She'd paid for her vacation in full, and no one was cutting it short. "My head is better. It still has a dull ache, but the intense throbbing is gone."

Zaire got to his feet. "Good to hear it." He cleared his throat. "Because of your illness, I'm paying one of my ranch hands to drive your car back to L.A. I'd like to fly you home first class. Please come back when you're one-hundred-percent. If you don't mind, I'll call and check on flights to Los Angeles. The airport isn't far away. I'll take you."

"Like hell you will," China shouted. "I'm not returning to L.A., not until my vacation is over. Then I'll drive myself back home. You've made a lot of assumptions. Wrong ones, I might add. If you think you can just swat me away like some pesky fly, you'd better think again. I'm staying put. Got it?"

"I'm only thinking of you, China. The ranch isn't a safe place for anyone who's sick. We're too far from the nearest hospital. I don't want to run the risk of you getting hurt or possibly becoming more burned-out than you already are."

"The last time I checked my birth certificate your name *was not* listed as my father. In fact, you're only making matters worse. I'm no pushover, and don't you forget it!"

"Has anyone ever told you you're stubborn and hard-headed?"

Beautiful and sexy to boot.

"Numerous times." Thrusting out her chin, China held her head high. "I guess no one has ever told you that you're just like me, obstinate and uncompromising."

"Hardly!"

Zaire knew he was in a no-win situation. China had decided she wasn't going anywhere, and he was sure no one could make her listen to reason. "Suit yourself." Huffily, he stormed toward the door. Before exiting, he turned and glanced back at her, then left the room.

Saddened and troubled by the heated exchange, China slid down in bed. She had overreacted—something she'd done a lot since her father's death. She wasn't leaving the ranch, so there was no use in her saying to Zaire that she was sorry.

However, she knew she should've accepted Zaire's sincere concern for her.

All she'd had to do was convince him she wanted to stay and rest. If nothing else, she could've told him she'd closely monitor her health—and if she didn't improve, she'd leave. Hindsight was always clear as sunlight. But it came only after creating a firestorm of unnecessary darkness. China knew she'd created the heat and firepower for this battle. It was a fight in which she could've easily waved a white flag of surrender.

Late the next morning, a knock on the door abruptly aroused China from a less-than-peaceful sleep. Getting out of bed, she located her robe and slipped it on. Making her way to the front door, she hoped it wasn't Zaire. She wasn't up for another battle with him. There was no fight left in her.

Bernice smiled softly at China. "I can see I woke you. I'm sorry. I was worried, so I dropped by to see how you're doing."

China opened the door wider. "Please come in. I could use a friend."

Bernice nodded, stepping inside. "I know how to be a friend. How *are* you?"

China had Bernice follow her back into the bedroom, gesturing for her to take the recliner. Climbing into the middle of the bed, she crossed her legs. "I guess Zaire told you what happened."

"He did."

Bernice's soothing voice put China at ease.

"He's concerned for your well-being, that's all. My sons don't like to see people suffer." Wanting her to understand Zaire, she told China how her husband had come back to her when he was sick and she had nursed him until he'd passed.

"As a nurse, I see suffering every day. It's something I've never gotten used to."

"It was awful for my boys watching their father suffer. They had such mixed emotions for the man who'd treated them so unkindly." Bernice laughed. "That last remark was truly an understatement my boys would call me on. As much at odds as they were with Macon, they couldn't keep compassion from ruling their kind hearts."

"I can imagine how hard it was on them. I pray I don't feel the same things if my mother ever comes back into my life. Has Zaire told you about my mother?"

"Not a single word. If you told him something in confidence, he'd never share it. Do you want to tell me about your mother?"

China smiled. "If it's a beautiful day outdoors it might ruin your mood."

"I'm strong. The beauty of the day will still be here for me. I learned long ago how to make the best of the worst. I've got too much to be grateful for."

China was amazed at Bernice's strong optimism. She was optimistic, too, just not all the time. She allowed darkness in more often than she should. After saying a silent prayer, she launched into the story of how her mother had left.

Listening with keen interest, Bernice watched the different expressions crossing China's pretty face. At the beginning of the story, she'd heard sadness in the young woman's voice. By the end of her tale, the bright rays of hope had burst through the darkness. "It's good you've accepted the situation for what it is. No longer blaming yourself for the mistakes of others is positive. I'm sure your dad was proud of you."

Grief tugging hard at her heartstrings, China laughed nervously. "He *was* very proud. He never let a day go by without telling me that and how much he loved me. His love helped shape me into the woman I am today. I'm not sure I would've gone to college and become a nurse without his encouragement and support."

"Life is interesting. It can also be extremely sad and funny. I did my best to rear my sons in a positive way. Things always went well with the boys and me. That is, until Macon got home from work. Then all hell broke loose around us."

"Ms. Bernice, you've succeeded with your sons. They've drawn a clear line in the sand when it comes to abuse. And they love their mother and aunts more than anything." Closing her eyes briefly, China silently prayed for inner peace. Bernice had already found it, and she wanted a wealth of it, too.

"Thanks for the warm praise. I'm extremely proud of them."

"Ms. Bernice, I feel much better. You *are* good for me. Thanks for coming out to see me. I'll talk to Zaire and raise the white flag. I hope he's not too mad."

Bernice got to her feet. "He's not mad, honey, just concerned. I may be stepping over the line here, but I believe Zaire cares for you more than as a ranch guest. Don't be too hard on him. He's a real good son, brother, nephew and brother-in-law. I just happen to think he wants a sweet girl to be a good man to. I won't call any names, but I think you just might know her pretty well."

China laughed softly. "If what you're saying is true, that makes two of us. Why else do you think I won't let him send me packing? Zaire has been good to me since I first got here. I'm not ready for our friendship to end so abruptly."

"Then don't let it." Bernice walked over to the bed and hugged China. "We'll talk. You already have my number. Don't hesitate to call. And don't get up. With your permission, I can put both locks back on."

"Thank you. Zaire gave me his cell number. Is this a good or bad time to call?"

Bernice winked. "The timing is perfect. Get some more rest. Sorry you're going to miss the baby shower later this evening."

A painful expression crossed China's features. "I don't want to miss it. Maybe I'll feel up to it by then. Where's it held?"

From the look on her face and the determination in her voice, China wasn't to be deterred. "The shower is at Hailey and Zurich's home at seven-thirty," Bernice answered. "Get as much rest as you can. If you feel up to it, let me know and I'll pick you up." Bernice waved as she left the room.

China heard the door close. She had her mind made up to ask his forgiveness. After dialing the first three numbers to Zaire's cell, she hung up. What she had to say should be said face-to-face. It would hopefully show Zaire how much she respected him.

Knowing she could use more sleep, China picked up the medicine bottle. Opening it, she shook out a single tablet, and downed it with water. Conceding to see the doctor if he came, China hoped she'd hear his knock. There was a doorbell outside, but thus far everyone was partial to rapping with bare knuckles.

Before the thought cleared China's head, a few sharp raps hit the door. Looking around for something heavier than her silk robe, she recalled hanging up a loose-fitting caftan. Rushing to retrieve it, slipping it on over her gown, she made a cautious journey toward the front.

Opening the door, China stood back and gave the man a good once-over.

Tipping his heather-gray Stetson, Dr. Jenkins removed it, revealing a shock of dark curls. He actually carried a black medical bag. "Good afternoon, Miss Braxton. I'm Dr. Harold Jenkins. Mr. Zaire Kingdom asked me to drop in and check out your physical condition. Is my visit okay with you?"

China smiled. "I was expecting you. Your timing is perfect. I was about to lie down and feared I might not hear the door." In one sweeping hand gesture, China approved Dr. Jenkins's entry. "Please, come in and have a seat."

The gentleman walked in and took a seat on the sofa. China sat in a nearby chair.

Dr. Jenkins was one good-looking black man, tall, built like a professional football player and solid as a rock. He had a deep Southern twang. As fine as he was to China, Zaire trumped him in every physical and facial feature.

Yes, Zaire infuriated her and made her crazy, but he had her wanting to spend every moment in his company.

"Mr. Kingdom explained what happened last evening. I'd like you to tell me your experience in your own words. No one but you can tell me how you felt and how you feel right now."

Sighing, China crossed her legs. "It was a migraine, Dr. Jenkins, combined with a bout of sheer fatigue. I've been running nonstop since my father's recent passing. I can't seem to wind down. The migraines began right after Dad's death. I have a prescription."

"I see. You have my condolences." He asked for information on her medication.

After giving the details, she continued. "This headache was my fourth or fifth in the past few weeks. By far, it was the worst. The throbbing pain was unrelenting, accompanied by nausea. It started around two this morning and didn't subside until I took the first dose of medicine. I've taken two single doses. One was taken just before you arrived."

Dr. Jenkins appeared impressed. "I wish all my patients could rattle off the important aspects of their illnesses and meds."

China laughed. "I'm a registered nurse."

"Ah, that certainly explains it. However, I know many nurses who can't do what you just did. It's like they forget their training altogether when they become patients."

"I know quite a few like that—my coworkers. We are some of the worst patients, but doctors are even worse."

Dr. Jenkins laughed. "I have to agree." He paused a moment. "I'd like to perform a preliminary exam. Okay with you?"

"No problem. Zaire won't be happy otherwise. He's trying to run me off the ranch because of the fainting spell.

I hope you can assure him I'm not at risk or a liability to his precious business."

"Mr. Kingdom is merely concerned. He expressed as much to me."

Opening his medical bag, Dr. Jenkins removed a pen-lightlike instrument, then walked over to China. "Please look straight ahead." Using the small instrument, he first examined her eyes. Afterward, he massaged her temples. "Does this hurt?"

China shook her head in the negative.

Satisfied with China's response, Dr. Jenkins checked her glands for any swelling. Once he'd pressed agile fingers in and around the areas of her neck, he checked her pulse. Taking her blood pressure twice, he monitored it closely. "Everything seems to be in order, young lady. Show me where you feel the most pain during a migraine."

"The intense throbbing is in my temples. Light is bothersome during more painful episodes."

"Those are typical migraine symptoms. I can clear you. I'll talk to Mr. Kingdom and let him know you're fit for duty," he joked. "I'd like to see you stay in bed and rest at least another day to deal with your severe exhaustion. Being overly tired can bring on all types of problems."

"I'm invited to a baby shower this evening. If I rest up until then, think I can attend for a couple of hours? It shouldn't be too exciting."

"It's too soon. You're very tired. Stay in bed the rest of the day. If you have another migraine, tell Mr. Kingdom to call me. I'm willing to come back to see you."

"I should be okay. The medicine normally works. Once I get enough rest and conquer my stress issues, I hope these migraines will stop. I didn't suffer them before my father's death. I'm assuming stressful grief is what caused them."

"You could be right. Monitor your health closely. I'm

leaving now. I hope the rest of your day will be pain-free. I'll give Mr. Kingdom a call once I get in the car."

China chuckled. "Do you always call the brothers Mr. Kingdom? It sounds so formal for people who have a working relationship. He has talked about you to me."

"I always show respect to families on professional duty calls. Off duty, other than Mr. and Mrs. Cobb and her sisters, it's just plain Zaire, Zurich and Zane. We've known each other most of our lives."

Even though China had had a pretty decent afternoon, and her head hadn't been hurting when she'd awakened around four o'clock in the afternoon, she'd called Ms. Bernice to voice her regret over not attending the shower. Total bed rest was the best thing for her.

China's mind had been on Zaire most of the morning and into the afternoon, wondering why he hadn't called or dropped by. She was sure he'd be at the shower, but she wanted to make up with him in private, not around his family.

A bout of anxiety suddenly attacked China.

What if Zaire refuses to see me?

How could she cope with the agony? If it went down that way, he'd have to tell her to her face. She was going to seek him out. However, she didn't feel so confident.

Anxiety often fueled hunger, which helped to keep her mind off of painful matters. Thinking about the plate of food Bernice had left on the table earlier, she got up and went to the kitchen.

Retrieving a paper plate and utensils, China speared a hamburger and a bun with her fork. With no chance of her kissing Zaire, she added a slice of onion to it.

After lathering the bun with mustard and mayonnaise, China filled a plastic cup with fruit punch. She moved over to the table and sat down. As soon as she finished eating, her thoughts went back to Zaire.

Zaire was a very real distraction for China, a hot and sexy diversion. Taking her mind off him wasn't going to be easy. She prayed he'd at least let her apologize to him.

Hoping to sway her mind away from Zaire, China began thinking about the baby shower. She hoped Hailey and Zurich received everything they needed for their unborn child. China was sorry she couldn't attend, but seeing Zaire alone was more appealing to her under the circumstances.

Zaire as a father came to mind. Someday he'd make a lucky woman an amazing husband. His children would no doubt get a loving, doting father. How did she know all this about a man she'd only met a short time ago? China felt it in her heart.

Clocks and work schedules had ruled China's everyday life for as long as she could remember…and she'd made a vow last night to try and ignore as many regimens as possible while on vacation. Since all ranch classes and activities were prescheduled, China couldn't completely get around setting the alarm.

China had taken a short walk right outside the cabin after she'd eaten. Shortly after her coming back inside, right after taking a hot shower a slight headache had developed just before she'd gotten into bed. Throughout the rest of the day and evening she had been at a total loss for something interesting to do. She still limited herself to only one pain pill and had slept soundly throughout the night.

On Monday morning, because of her refusal to set the alarm clock, she slept late. Missing yesterday's baby shower had taxed China in a way she hadn't expected. Disappointment had settled in. She hadn't done a single strenuous thing, but she'd felt totally worn down by bedtime.

* * *

Shortly after the lunch hour, wearing mint-green jeans and a white-and-mint-colored short-sleeved camp shirt, China made her way from the parking lot to the ranch's nearby dining hall. She hoped against hope to find Zaire there, having longed to see him throughout the previous day. Being ignored by him hurt her something awful, yet she still planned to ask his forgiveness.

It was impossible to speak to an invisible man yet China spoke to him through her heart, quietly rehearsing what she'd say with humility. Would Zaire be willing to take his precious time to listen? China knew she'd been overly obstinate with him. All he was guilty of was showing concern for her.

Zaire stepped out of the dining hall door. Spotting China, his long strides came to an abrupt halt. Shading his eyes, he watched her advancing figure, delighting in the view. He couldn't see her facial features clearly, but he saw she had more pep in her step.

China moving around so well lifted Zaire's spirits. Since he'd last seen her, he hadn't been able to think of anything but her and their heated exchange. He blamed himself for some of what had occurred, yet he didn't hold China completely blameless. Her stubbornness had started it, yet he'd kept it going by getting into an argument he'd had no chance of winning in the first place. Then he'd totally ignored her so they didn't get into another verbal scrimmage.

"Hi, Zaire. Glad I caught up with you." She extended her hand to him. "I apologize for acting out the way I did the last time I saw you. I take full responsibility for what happened between us. I had hoped to talk to you before now."

Zaire grinned. Cautiously, briefly, he took her extended

hand, wanting to kiss the back of it. "I'm willing to share the blame. Both of us were way out of line. You look great, and I hope your headaches and fatigue have disappeared. Have they?"

China smiled. "Both have calmed down quite a bit." She shuffled her feet nervously. "I'm passing on riding lessons for another day or so, but I'd like to see you. Can I interest you in dinner in town this evening? I'd love to show my appreciation for your concern."

If appreciation was the only reason she had for inviting him to dinner, Zaire's head shouted for him to turn her down. "What time, China?" His heart clearly didn't agree with his mindset. He was unable to resist his wild desire to be back in her company.

"I normally eat dinner around six-thirty. Is that okay?"

"Whatever time you decide on is fine by me."

"Six-thirty, it is. Do you have a favorite restaurant?"

"I love dining at Salt Grass Steakhouse. It's only fifteen minutes away."

"Good. I'll pick you up here at six."

China had just invited the man of her deepest desires to dinner, the sexy man who lit a fire under her. "Is your mother inside?"

Zaire nodded. "Lunch is over, but she's in the kitchen before and after any scheduled meal. She'll be happy to see you looking so well." After moving only a few steps away, he stopped. "By the way, *can* you cook?"

"Maybe you'll get a chance to see, corporate cowboy."

Smiling sweetly, China saluted Zaire. "See you later."

Tipping his hat, he nodded, smiling back. "Later."

A great idea zipped through China's head as she quickly made her way toward the kitchen. Realizing she was moving a bit too fast, she slowed down, not wanting a thing to get in the way of the fantastic evening she wanted to plan. As thoughts of sweet romance crowded out everything else, sexual heat swelled inside her femininity.

"Let it come as it may, China Doll," she said softly.

Chapter 5

Bernice was talking to an employee when China burst into the kitchen. Holding up a finger, the Kingdom family matriarch let her know she'd be a moment.

Spotting a metal table and two chairs over in a corner, China walked across the room and sat down. Looking around the kitchen, she tapped on her thighs with the tips of her nails.

Bernice pulled out a chair and sat across from her guest. "My dear, you're looking much better. In fact, you're glowing today. Lunch is over, but I can fix you a plate. Foods are still piping hot."

Smiling gently, China shook her head. "Thanks, but I'm not here to eat. I need your advice." She paused a moment. "I invited Zaire out to dinner this evening, but when he asked me if I could cook, I saw it as a challenge to show him. But I don't even know where a grocery store is. Can you tell me where to find a market near here?"

Bernice laughed. "You're sitting in the middle of one. If we don't have it in stock, it's probably unobtainable. What are you thinking of preparing?"

"I don't know." China shrugged. "What's Zaire's favorite dish?"

"Beef stew, my dear. Even though the weather is hot, Zaire can eat stew for breakfast, lunch and dinner. Fortunately, I have lots of tender beef on hand."

Pleased, China smiled. "Do you have a recipe I can follow?"

"I don't measure. I follow my instincts. Maybe you should try it. Beef stew is easy to make. Do you know what goes in it?"

Pushing her hands through her hair, China blinked. "Beef, of course." She thought back on her dad making the dish to use up leftover meat and vegetables. "I recall Dad putting onions and potatoes in a pot. Besides that, I'm clueless."

"Sliced fresh carrots and chopped celery are great ingredients. Beef broth or a few beef bouillon cubes will enrich your soup base. Let me get together the ingredients and spices. I'll label what's in each plastic baggie."

China raised a questioning eyebrow. "What else goes with stew?"

"It's a meal in itself, child. Zaire is big on fresh garden salad. Don't worry, China, I'll help you out."

"Thanks, Ms. Bernice." China paused a moment. "Do you think I'm making a big mistake inviting Zaire to dinner in the cabin? Is it too suggestive?"

"Not at all, China. Shy men need a little push for encouragement. If Zaire wasn't interested in dinner, he would've said so. Change of venue won't be a problem for him."

"Thanks again. Do you think I should tell him I asked you about cooking or just not mention it?"

"Tell him. Our family doesn't keep secrets. Enough of that went on when the boys were small. They're men now. Secrets are a destructive force."

China nodded in agreement. "That's a good description. I'm sorry I asked the question. You guys are wonderful. I love the way you operate as a family."

Bernice stood. "Let me get what you'll need so you can be on your way. Beef stew doesn't take long to make. Prepare the beef first. Cook it until it is tender enough to cut with a fork."

Gratitude gleamed in China's eyes. "I'm confident I can pull it off. I plan to stop at the gift shop and pick up a few candles." China winked. "I want to put Zaire in a relaxed mood."

Bernice chuckled. "Go on over to the gift shop while I get your package ready."

Worn out from running around in what seemed like all the wrong directions, China finally dropped down on the sofa. Glancing over at the lovely table she'd set for two, she smiled, hoping Zaire would be pleased with the change in plans.

A pillar candle nesting inside fresh flowers served as a centerpiece. Bernice had told her about a field of colorful blossoms growing wild behind the cottages. She had picked a couple of dozen blooms and had gathered several twigs to twist and bind together to create a unique design.

The CD player was stacked with a variety of discs featuring slow, mellow Country-Western songs. She was careful to stay away from the somebody-did-me-wrong-themed songs. There was enough sadness in the world; she didn't need to hear pain in her music.

The lineup included LeAnn Rimes, Faith Hill, Reba McEntire, Randy Travis, Tim McGraw and Clint Black.

China sniffed the air. The beef stew smelled great. She hoped it'd taste just as good. Although she planned to sample it before serving it to Zaire, she had no way of comparing her taste buds to his.

Sure that her clothing smelled like onions and spices, she got up from the sofa and headed toward the bathroom. China gave a minute of thought to what perfume she might wear for a special evening. It was going to be a great night.

Zaire was not only pleased by the change in venue and delicious smells wafting across his nose, but he also loved China's sexy white dress. Short, with puffed sleeves and a low-cut bodice, the pure cotton sheath perfectly fit her petite figure. He also liked her dainty white ballet slippers.

"You're beautiful, China Doll."

China blushed heavily, her eyes scanning Zaire. He'd swapped his trademark denims for dark gray, neatly pressed dress slacks. A white summer-weight polo sweater had replaced his Western-style shirt. An expensive-looking gray Stetson with a white leather band rested on the sofa's arm.

China's eyes connected with Zaire's. "Thanks for the compliment. Have a seat at the table, Zaire. I hope you're good and hungry."

Zaire chuckled. "I can assure you I'll do the meal justice. I'm a big man with a big appetite." He pulled out two chairs at the same time. "Can I help you with anything before I sit down?"

China smiled warmly. "I've got it under control. Just relax. Everything will be on the table in a jiffy. Iced tea or lemonade?"

"If you don't mind, a glass of each works fine. Both are favorites."

"Don't mind it at all. I'll take care of it. I fixed one of your favorites, beef stew. I know it won't taste as good as your mom's, but it's good. I sampled it already. Hope you enjoy it."

Zaire lifted an eyebrow. "Bernice Kingdom-Cobb is letting you in on my secrets, isn't she? I need to have a mother-son chat with her."

"She only told me your favorite dish because I asked. In fact, I think she's very discreet…and she's extremely proud of her three fine sons."

Zaire chuckled. "I know Mom won't ever break a confidence. None of us are into that sort of thing."

"Good! Excuse me a moment, Zaire. I'll be right back."

Feeling the blushing heat on her cheeks, China rushed into the kitchen.

Reappearing in a matter of seconds, she set down a borrowed soup tureen filled with beef stew. Turning right around, she went back for corn-bread muffins and a glass dish of soft butter. Bernice had thought of everything China wouldn't have.

Taking her seat at the table, China bowed her head and said a blessing. Amen was voiced simultaneously.

China spread out a napkin on her lap. "Dad taught me how to fix homemade muffins and a variety of other baked goods. Some things I cook better than others."

Zaire nodded. "That's how it is with most of us. The Kingdom men had no choice but to learn to cook. Mom never wanted to worry about us going hungry. She was always confident we'd achieve enough success to make adequate money to feed ourselves. Learning to fix simple meals eventually made us want to tackle elaborate ones. If you didn't notice, we like challenges. There aren't too many meals we don't know how to fix."

China appeared impressed. "I like challenges, too. Asking if I could cook was what prompted the change in plans. I hope you enjoy everything. I wanted to show my appreciation for your kindnesses, but it's also my way of apologizing for how badly I've acted. I'm sorry, Zaire. I could've handled our earlier problem with some diplomacy. I was downright tactless."

Hearing deep regret in her voice, Zaire's eyes brimmed with understanding. "We were both short on self-discipline that day. I'm sure we'd do differently if we had a chance to do it over. Now that we've voiced our regrets…it's over."

Pressing two fingers to her lips, China blew Zaire a kiss. "Thank you."

After dipping up several ladles of stew and transferring it to his bowl, Zaire scooped up some rich broth in his soupspoon and tasted it. As though he was surprised, his eyebrows lifted appreciatively. "The stew tastes as good as Mom's." Biting off half a corn-bread muffin, he practically inhaled it. "The muffins are light and flaky. Everything is flavorful. Is it your first time fixing beef stew?"

"Yes." China brightened. "I'm relieved you like it."

Zaire pursed his lips. "When you'd mentioned showing appreciation earlier, I was of a mind to turn you down if it was your only reason for inviting me. I'm happy to be joining you for a nice, quiet evening. If we do this again, I hope it occurs simply because we both want it to." He stared into her eyes. "Did I make myself plain enough?"

"Plain as the nose on your face." A nervous China rubbed her hands up and down her arms. "I tend to like folks who are direct and right to the point."

"I like frankness in people, too. That is, in some instances."

Curiosity settled in China's eyes. "When *doesn't* it work for you?"

"During heated arguments, when I'm being chewed out," Zaire confessed. "I don't like confrontations. I spent my entire youth in the midst of horrible altercations, where someone usually got physically hurt. Mom received the brunt of Macon's alcohol-induced rages. But emotional bruising was a daily occurrence for us all. I left the city for the same reasons. Many top-brass employees were often confrontational."

Tears filled China's eyes. "I'm sorry, Zaire, sorry I made you feel so bad. I promise to be mindful of your feelings on confrontation. Normally I'm not angry or rude. My mouth got carried away because I felt you were forcing me into something I was against. I don't like being told what to do."

Reaching out to her, Zaire briefly covered China's hand with his own. "I'm not a forceful person by any stretch of the imagination. Sorry if I gave that impression. I realize confrontation is natural between friends, lovers and family, but too much of it isn't good. It's damaging to the spirit. Everything I did and said earlier was out of genuine care and concern for you. Think we can put the episode behind us and start fresh?"

China smiled brightly. "I can't think of any reason why not."

Zaire's eyes softened. "I like you, China, a lot. I'm interested in building a friendship with you." He looked down momentarily. "I have to be honest here. I've been hoping for more than a friendly liaison, though I'm not sure how realistic that is. How much more do I want?" He shrugged. "I have no clue. Maybe we can figure it out together."

Pleasure burst loose inside China's heart, making her feel champagne-bubbly. "I think that's a great idea. However, we're running out of time. I'm only here for two weeks. Nearly three days of my vacation is gone."

"Let's play it by ear and see what happens. We don't have to figure out everything right this minute."

China smiled. "I agree. Let's finish dinner before everything gets cold."

Zaire was never forward or blunt with women. Tongue-tied and shy was more like it. Something about China challenged him to do things he'd only dreamed of. She filled him up with all kinds of emotions, inspiring him, making him want to feel again. Zaire wanted to learn how to love China Braxton.

As they began eating again, Zaire stole covert glances at China every few seconds. He couldn't stop thinking of how much she intrigued him. He was worried he might've said too much already. A man telling a woman he liked her could either thrill her or give her absolute chills. China gave him both thrills and chills, but each excited him in a deliciously wonderful way.

The soft music playing kept total silence at bay.

Through with his meal, Zaire stood and began cleaning off the table.

"Don't worry about the dishes. I'll get everything done later," China remarked.

"We can do it together if you'd like."

Do it together.

Giggling inwardly at her naughty thoughts, China quickly turned away her face so Zaire wouldn't see the huge smile he'd put there. Would they ever *do it?* she wondered. Such juvenile terminology, she thought.

Making love is a more appropriate phrase. Would we ever make love? Yes, most definitely, even if it only occurs in my wildest fantasies.

Resting his chin atop China's head, Zaire danced with her over the small area of the living room. After he'd learned she also loved the group Rascal Flatts, he'd gone out to his truck to get their latest CD.

Inhaling the delectable coconut scent of her hair, he

closed his eyes. "You feel good in my arms. Are you comfortable?"

China giggled. "Comfortable may not be the right word. I'm in heaven, Zaire. Being in your arms is just like I've imagined. We've slow danced before, but I was scared to think of us in a romantic way then. I'm not fearful anymore."

Nuzzling her neck with his nose, her tantalizing scent lit a fire in his loins, making him want her in the worst way. China's hand squeezing him ever so gently had suddenly stymied his thought process.

Removing Zaire's hands from her shoulders, China placed them around her waist and drew her body in closer to his. Looking up into his eyes, she smiled softly. "Would you think I was too forward if I told you I'm turned on by your touch?"

Zaire laughed. "Holding you close to me is the only thing on my mind and I definitely don't think I'm too forward. Would you consider it an unwanted advance if I tasted your tender lips?"

China stifled a gasp. "Try it and see." Looking up at him, she batted her lashes, flirting openly. "Need any more encouragement?"

Lowering his head until their mouths met, Zaire gently traced the curve of China's full lower lip with his own. Looking into her eyes, cupping her face in both his hands, he hungrily sought out her mouth, kissing her the way a man and woman linked by fiery passion would kiss. He instantly felt the sweet drugging sensations.

Deepening the kiss caused a flaring firestorm inside Zaire's belly, not to mention the erotic effect it had on his manhood. If her desires matched his, she wanted relentless kisses, sweet, hot, wet and insanely passionate.

The slow song played on. Other than hungry mouths

moving with feral urgency, their bodies had come to a complete standstill. Lifting China into his arms, Zaire danced her over to the CD player, where he turned up the music.

In the next second, shocking her senseless, Zaire carried her out the front door, leaving it open so the music could be heard. Stepping off the porch, he set her on her feet and resumed dancing. After briefly looking up at the star-dusted skies, China's head went straight to Zaire's broad chest.

Feeling how fast his heart raced made her smile, causing her hand to tenderly rove over his chest. Glad she had the same effect on him that he had on her, she grinned. Her rapidly beating heart hadn't slowed one bit since he'd first taken her into his arms. Their hearts seemed to beat in perfect harmony.

Starting to feel he was in over his head, Zaire put a slight distance between them. "I hope I'm not moving too fast. I don't want to scare you."

China's smile was faint. "You're not scaring me…and you won't. Let's just concentrate on having a good time, Zaire. It'd be a shame to allow fear to keep us from getting to know each other."

Smiling softly, Zaire pointed up at the moon. "We have lots of moonlight so let's make the best of it." He held her closer. Using an open palm, he tenderly guided her head back to his chest. Zaire closed his eyes. Clean air filled his nostrils and he relaxed, resting his chin atop her head. Committed to living each tantalizing moment one second at a time, his mouth silently formed a vow to spend lots of quality time with China.

Back inside, China turned on the electric fireplace. Just for the light show, she told herself. No romantic notions. She couldn't help wondering what the ranch was like during Thanksgiving, Christmas and New Year's Eve. Knowing

Bernice as she did, the entire place would be colorful and festive.

Looking over at Zaire, she was pleased by how comfortable he looked. Walking into the kitchen, she turned on the burner beneath the stainless teakettle. While digging around in a ceramic jar, she came up with several types of tea bags. Settling on cinnamon for her hot drink, she leaned against the counter and cleared her throat to catch Zaire's attention. "What type of tea do you want?"

"Orange spice. It's too late for coffee."

China smiled. "I just happen to like orange spice, too."

Looking over at the clock, China scowled. Knowing Zaire had an early wake-up call had her wishing it wasn't so. She didn't want to keep him out too late, but she didn't want him to leave either.

"Stop worrying about the time. No matter how late I get to bed, I get up on time."

Hating the color flooding into her cheeks, China wondered how he'd read her mind. "I'm not worried about you getting up on time."

"Yes you are. It's written all over your face. In case you haven't noticed, I'm a rather big boy, Ms. Braxton. I'll leave in a few minutes so you won't have to be concerned about me missing my morning gigs."

"No, no, I'm not concerned," she said too quickly, wishing he hadn't read her.

Zaire busted up laughing. "You are so transparent. That's okay, though. I like it."

Rushing across the room, Zaire pulled China into his arms, kissing her cheeks. "You are too precious for words. Embarrassing you is really easy. I may have to teach you how to grow a thicker skin." He laughed at her expression of feigned suffering.

China smiled her best one for Zaire. Carrying a hot mug

of tea into the living room, she set it down on a coaster on the coffee table. After retrieving her cup, she pulled out the raisin-oatmeal cookies Ms. Bernice had given her.

Zaire's eyes brightened at the sight of the sweets. "You made these?"

"I wish. Your mom gave them to me."

"In that case, I know they're delicious. I heard you say you bake, but what about cookies?" Dropping down on the sofa, he helped himself to his mom's baked goods.

Following his lead, China sat down, too, putting a respectable distance between them, despite the light intimacy they'd shared. "I do chocolate chip and sugar cookies, but I don't bake often. It's impossible to fix only a few. You have to do a couple dozen or more. Once in a while, when I'm in the mall, I stop and get a couple of cookies to munch on."

China and Zaire took time out of conversing to sip their tea, blowing on the hot drinks before tasting.

"You have a lot of chores around here, but what do you do for fun, Zaire? How do you let your hair down?"

Smoothing his hand over his head, he laughed. "With such a close haircut, there's not much to let down." He looked closely at her. "Everything I do on the ranch is enjoyable for me, even the heavier chores. Teaching others my God-given skills is about as fun as it gets. Seeing the smile on a child's face once they take the first solo lap around the ring on horseback is thrilling for me. These are the same activities that once kept my mind off home turmoil. Riding and roping and fishing were my escapes from the hell we endured. Even my studies brought me pleasure. It wasn't just my escape either. Zurich and Zane had the same getaways."

"How was it for you after Zurich left for prep school?"

"Tough, but Zane and I still had each other. I thank God Dad had already left when I had to leave Zane to attend

Buckley Academy. I'm not sure I would've left if he'd still been here. Our baby brother didn't grow tall and strong as quickly as Zurich and me. He was a lightweight. Zurich and I were his only protectors."

"How old were you when Macon left home?"

"Thirteen. We found out later that he didn't leave voluntarily. Morgan and his buddies ran him off, telling him he'd get hurt real bad if he didn't disappear. Macon was a lot of things, but he wasn't a fool, not in that sense. He took the threats seriously. Don't know if Morgan and his boys would've hurt Macon, but they railroaded him right out of town. Another sad day for us was when he came back. Ill and broken down, he begged Mom to take him back in. She did, without hesitation."

"Did they live as husband and wife?"

"Mom was his nurse, friend and confidante, but she didn't share his bed. As a Christian woman, she took her vows seriously. Until death do us part was how it was for her. Morgan had tried to get her to divorce Macon and marry him before Dad came back. She'd tell us divorce was against God's law. She knows better now."

China frowned. "What do you mean?"

"Morgan read her God's plan for divorce in the Bible. According to her, he broke it down real good, explaining God's meaning of an ungodly man. However, that didn't happen until Macon was already in the house. My aunts tried to talk Mom out of taking him in, but no one could convince her otherwise. Saint Bernice, as we fondly call her, stuck to her spiritual calling."

"She's downright miraculous if you ask me. Were you guys angry with her?"

Zaire shook his head. "For what? We knew who our mother was better than anyone. She'd take care of the red-headed devil if called upon. She's a servant of God. As a pure-hearted humanitarian, she did what she felt was right."

China could tell by Zaire's body language that he was growing tired of this particular conversation. The evening was supposed to be a relaxing one. She decided to suspend the heavy grilling and allow him to recapture his peace.

Surprising China, Zaire grabbed a pillow and positioned it on her lap. Stretching out fully, he laid his head on the pillow and looked up at her. "What made you decide to become a nurse?"

"Sick people."

Zaire laughed heartily. "That's a good enough reason. Was there an experience of some kind or a particular illness that stood out for you?"

"Nothing specific. I used to go see the school nurse all the time for the least ache or pain. It was my way of getting out of class, but I liked the nurses I had in high school. They were kind and understanding, but it was Nurse Patterson who told me I needed to stop coming to the nurse's office without just cause. She explained that I was stealing time away from authentically sick students with my bogus illnesses. I felt guilty."

"She busted you, huh?"

"Yeah, I'm not sure it would've impacted me so greatly earlier. Faking sick made me feel horrible as a teenager. I remember after one visit for cramps, Nurse Patterson showed me on the calendar how I'd had three menstrual cycles in a single month. Boy did that revelation hit home!"

Zaire laughed. "I'm glad you found your calling, no matter how it came about. Nursing is an extremely important profession. All nurses should be proud of their work."

"Thanks for the kudos. I love my job. There are so many people who need our medical services. More than that, they need understanding, tons of love and compassion. Many of my elderly patients remain close to me. I check on them often and I try to share in their special events, such as birthdays. I can't tell you how many of these ladies and gentlemen came to my aid when Dad passed away."

"It sounds like they're in pretty good shape."

"They suffer from all kinds of diseases, diabetes to cancer," China said with some sadness. "But you know what? These people have found a reason to keep on living. I have a former male patient who is eighty-seven. Glenn was baptized a couple of months ago for the first time ever. I attended his baptism, along with several others from our little group. I've introduced many of my friends, who are also my patients, to each other. Age difference doesn't matter. We have fun getting together on a regular basis."

"Where do you and your patients meet up?"

"We use a senior center and a local church banquet hall. Sometimes we go out to a restaurant if everyone is up to it. There's a middle-aged couple with a van, the Hanks. They gladly pick up everyone who's without transportation. We have a ball."

He grinned. "You all seem to have a great time together." He stole a glance at his watch. "This has been fun, but I'd better mosey on home. I like to be at my best at work. Guests deserve one-hundred-percent from us. Mind walking me out?"

China stood and casually looped her arm through his. "Thanks for coming. I really enjoyed our evening. You're a lot of fun to hang out with."

Zaire kissed her forehead. "So are you. Thanks for having me over. The beef stew was very good, and the company was fantastic. What are your plans for tomorrow?"

China shrugged. "I'm not sure yet. I plan to take another look at the activity schedule before I go to bed. I do want to get up super early and spread some of Dad's ashes. I can't keep putting it off. I should've gotten started on the fishing expedition."

Sympathy was in Zaire's eyes as he looked into China's. "Want some company?"

She shook her head. "No. I should do it alone. I still talk to Dad like he's here with me. It may get a little emotional if I start telling him how much he's missed."

"I'm sure it will." Zaire gently stroked her arm, his sad face and watery eyes revealing how desperately he wanted to be there for her. "It's why I offered to tag along."

"Thanks, but I'll get through it. I'll probably have some things to say to Dad that should be said privately. If you get a moment, will you give me a call tomorrow?"

Zaire frowned, his dismay apparent. "I respect your decision to go it alone. If you change your mind, call. As for communicating tomorrow, I'll create time. We'll talk."

Chapter 6

An hour and a half before sunrise, China headed toward the Lake of Whispers, the body of water located only a few yards from her cabin. In the fold of her arm, wrapped in a blanket, she carried a brass-and-copper urn with Brody's ashes inside. Thinking about the sorrowful task at hand, she shivered.

As Zaire came to mind, China wished she'd taken him up on his offer. Telling him she had to do this alone hadn't placated him one bit, but he had respected her decision. As they'd walked out last night, he'd said his concern hadn't been about her walking around by herself in the wee hours of the morning. Being alone in her sorrow was what worried him most. He'd told her he knew how easily grief could suddenly rush a heart and overwhelm the spirit.

China carefully unfurled the blanket from around the urn. Holding the cool metal up to her mouth, she kissed it. "We're here at the Lake of Whispers. Your spirit has already been returned to God, but now I'll spread the first of your ashes over the water, just as you wanted me to do." While inching her way closer to the water's edge, China's hands trembled hard.

After removing the vacuum-sealed top, she practiced extreme caution with the container to keep from dropping it. Once she poured a handful of ashes into her left palm, she cautiously resealed the top.

Moving closer to the water, China flung open her hand. Through a blur of tears, she watched ashes flying freely over the lake. "Eternity is yours, as you rest in peace in your native Texas. Daddy, I love you."

The unexpected feel of tender hands upon her shoulders instantly soothed China. She felt Zaire's warmth, smelled his clean scent. Glad he had ignored her wish of going this alone, she rested her head back against his chest. "Thank you," she whispered softly. "Thank you for sensing my need for you when these stubborn lips refused to admit it."

Zaire kissed the top of her head. "You're welcome. Are you okay?"

"Under the circumstances, I'm as well as I can be. I miss him," she said, her voice cracking. "It's hard waking up every morning knowing I have to face the day without him. I thought he'd always be here with me and for me."

"He is, China Doll." Reaching his hand down to her heart, he massaged it gently. "Dads *are* forever. As mean as Macon was to us, he'll always be our dad."

"You've lost a father, too. It doesn't matter that our experiences were totally different. Like you said, dads are forever."

"This is your time to grieve. I came here hoping to help you find solace."

"Mission accomplished." Fully letting go of her emotions, China sobbed hard.

Zaire turned her to face him, pressing her head against his chest. "Go ahead and cry it out. It'll take a lot of tears to flood this big, strong chest."

Zaire's soothing words made China sob even harder. She'd tried so often to avoid her grief, but it only made her more miserable. This man holding her in his arms gave her the freedom and courage to let go. China was sure she'd cry over her father's demise for the rest of her life, but she was grateful she wasn't alone now. Zaire was there for her.

Zaire picked up the blanket and spread it out on the ground. He sat and guided China down to him. Stretching out fully, he brought her head against his chest once again. "In a short while, it'll be daylight. You and I are going to celebrate the sunrise."

China wiped her tears. "That sounds nice. Daddy and I loved to watch sunrises. We used to set our alarms to make sure we got up in time to witness it."

Zaire gently stroked her hair and tenderly massaged her back. "What's your sweetest memory of your dad?"

Sitting halfway up, China leaned her head on Zaire's shoulder and swallowed the lump in her throat. "Speaking of sweet, I'd have to say it was the sweet sixteen birthday party he threw for me. How he'd managed to keep it a complete secret was a miracle. My best girlfriend, Brooke, had assisted Dad in inviting friends he didn't know. My sixteenth birthday was spectacular—and so was my dad."

More tears rolling down her face, China lay back on the blanket, sliding her hand into Zaire's. "There are so many memories of Brody Braxton locked inside my heart. I was very much a Daddy's girl…and I didn't care who knew it."

Zaire leaned over and hugged China. "Your memories of Mr. B. will protect you and keep your heart warm forever." Lifting the ends of the blanket, Zaire folded it around her.

"In a few more minutes, the sun will invade the sky. Are you ready for it?"

China smiled softly. "Sharing a sunrise with you is a bonus I hadn't counted on. Thanks for being here."

"Thanks for not sending me away. My heart just couldn't stand you doing this alone."

Flat on their backs, heads touching, looking up at the sky, China and Zaire watched as the bright yellow sun slowly made its grand entrance. He whistled softly and China sighed with reverence. It was a magical moment, an unforgettable one.

As China began to relax, Zaire positioned himself on the blanket until their arms touched. His first class began at seven, less than an hour from then. If he had it his way, he'd spend the entire day just lying there with China, looking up at the sky. But the ranch wouldn't run itself.

Feeling Zaire so close to her made China's body tingle. The heated vibes between them were strong. She'd never felt so safe and secure with any man besides her father. Zaire wanted more than friendship out of this relationship—and so did she. Unfortunately, her vacation would have to end.

Zaire pulled himself straight up. "As much as I hate this to end, I have to go. I can't make my class wait." Leaning over her, he lowered his head and kissed her lips tenderly. "Do you have plans for this evening?"

"Not really. This afternoon I'm taking the hour-long beginning guitar class your stepfather teaches. After that, I'm free as a bird."

"If you haven't heard about it, there's a bonfire tonight for all guests. There'll be games, music and roasting hot dogs and marshmallows over open fires. I'd love for us to go together."

"You just landed yourself a bonfire partner, Mr. Kingdom. What time?"

"I'll pick you up around seven. There'll be lots of other activities for everyone to take part in. It's a real fun time."

"After such a sorrowful beginning to the day, I'm up for fun. Thanks for inviting me." Taking the initiative to get what she wanted, she kissed him gently on the mouth.

Pleased by her sweet kiss, Zaire closed his eyes, enjoying the fiery sensations galloping throughout his body. Her kiss ended and his imagination took over.

Hating to go, Zaire finally got to his feet. "Before you leave the ranch, maybe we can take a ride into Brownsville or down to South Padre Island for dinner. Interested?"

"Very much so, Zaire. Either one or both is fine with me. I'd love to sun on the beach. Maybe I can sign up for the next day trip there."

"I want us to drive down independent of the group. Do you mind that?"

China laughed. "Are you kidding? I'd love it."

"Me, too." He brought her into his arms and kissed her again.

Before going back inside the cabin, China faced front to look out over the ranch. Trees were in abundance, but only because the Kingdoms had had them planted everywhere. Miles and miles of white fencing served as visible borders, contributing to the picturesque country setting. According to what Zaire had said, before construction had begun, the ranch had simply been acre after acre of undeveloped land, overrun with tumbleweed and other dry shrubbery and an occasional tree here and there.

Whispering Lakes Ranch was a well-known address in a rustic paradise. What she experienced had been birthed by the man she was falling in love with. His family and other professionals had helped bring his dream to life, but he was the man behind the dream.

China dropped down onto the front porch swing. *Falling in love? Me? Yes, you,* she responded. *If there's a finer man out there in the world for me, I haven't met him yet. Zaire Kingdom is exactly the kind of man Brody Braxton would approve of, and he seems to be the same kind of man I've dreamed of. He's honest, compassionate and caring. And he loves his mother. I may be wrong, but I think he's special. I know many men, and only the taken ones have exhibited this kind of character.*

We live so far apart. I love the city. It's all I've known, yet I'm so comfortable in this place Zaire loves deeply. Is it possible for our two worlds to merge?

Getting up from the wooden swing, China finally made her way into the cabin. Since Zaire had helped her tidy up the kitchen last night, the only chores left would be done by the maid service sometime between eight and nine this morning.

Since her first class wasn't until after lunch, she decided to relax on the swing with a good book. Because of all the emotionally exhausting events of the day, she needed to take everything slow and easy.

Dressed in white shorts, a red tank top and barefooted, China lay atop a blanket she'd spread out on the cushioned swing. The air was perfectly still, and the trees were free of rustling. Just beyond the large pool area, the land was dry and sandy-like.

Having a hard time keeping her eyes open, China laid aside the book and closed her eyes. The swing was comfortable, strong and sturdy. Within the next few minutes she fell into a peaceful slumber.

* * *

If she'd awakened ten to fifteen minutes later, China would've been late for the guitar class. She was kind of surprised to see only fifteen or so students present, especially since all other classes she'd participated in had been fuller.

Walking across the modest-size room, China took a seat in the front row. She liked to be up front in any class she signed up for so she wouldn't miss a thing. Other students were spaced out in the rows of chairs and no one appeared crowded. China noticed that several people held instruments. Probably privately owned, she assumed.

Smiling broadly, Zaire sauntered into the classroom and made his way to a podium in the front of the room. "Hello, class. It's nice to see you. For those of you who haven't met me, I'm Zaire Kingdom, co-owner of the ranch. I know the guitar instructor was listed as Morgan Cobb, but he and I swapped classes. At my request, I must say. I had a particular reason for wanting to instruct this class."

Looking right at China, Zaire's eyes drank in as much of her as possible. Then he winked. He seemed not to care who may've noticed his flirtatious antics. It looked to him as if the sun had been busy caressing her bare flesh, toasting it to a golden brown. Texas sun could also easily burn the flesh, so he made a mental note to tell her to be careful.

China was so cute and adorable. He chuckled under his breath, wondering what she'd do if he walked over there and kissed her in front of everyone. Zaire suddenly rubbed his cheek in an effort to bring himself back to his senses.

"How many are beginners on the guitar?" Zaire asked.

China and three other participants raised hands. All beginners exchanged warm smiles of understanding, establishing themselves as comrades.

"Who are the intermediates?" Five or six students put

up their hands. "Deducting the beginners and intermediates, it appears we have several advanced students present. Welcome to each of you. For those of you who don't have a guitar," Zaire said, "please come and select one you'd like to use. Try on several for size. Test them out for weight and comfort. Some are much heavier than others. Beginners, I suggest using the lighter ones. Once you've made your choices, everyone can return to their seats and we'll get started."

Zaire walked over to the side of the room, where several acoustic guitars were laid out on a wide ledge covered with a velvet-soft material.

Zaire once again proved himself a patient man. "Not everyone can read music," he mentioned, "but it'll be helpful if you learn at some point. Lots of people who can't read music play instruments, so don't get thrown off course. The main chords will be taught in this class. Please use your picks, unless you want bruised fingers before the end of our first session."

Breathless was always how Zaire made China feel. She hadn't expected him to teach this class, but she was ecstatic over it. *At my request,* she recalled him saying. It was a deliciously juicy thought.

All that mattered to China was his charming, irresistible presence. Thinking about their next kiss filled her with joy.

A young lady held up her hand. "How much do you think we'll know about playing the guitar by the final class?"

"That will vary by individual. If you follow my instructions, first-time students should be able to strum a few simple songs when the classes are over. Feel free to ask any questions that come to mind. For advanced students, I'd appreciate it if you'd pair up with beginners or intermediates to offer guidance and helpful tips. Don't get worried and uptight. These classes are meant to be fun. Stay relaxed."

* * *

China left the classroom feeling way more confident about actually learning to play the guitar than she had before going inside. She walked out into the sunlight and stared up at the bright sky.

The weather was too hot and muggy for her liking. She closed her eyes and imagined swimming in the waters of a Southern California beach. Venice Beach was closest to where she lived. It was one of the cleaner ones and she loved to hang out there. It was a touristy place but it was also a fun hot spot for local residents. The crazy things going on there rarely happened in other oceanside cities. Los Angeles and its beach towns were in her DNA. Loving her home came naturally to her.

On Friday, the end of China's first week, a tour bus would take guests to beaches at South Padre Island. She wasn't sure it'd be a pleasant experience, not if it was as hot as it was today. The island was farther south, right at the Mexican border, which meant higher temperatures. The beach waters should make it somewhat cooler, she thought.

"End of the week is the future. This is today. Live in the moment, girl," she told herself. She hadn't felt this carefree since before Brody's passing. China somehow got the feeling her daddy was watching over her.

Zaire rushed up and startled her, making her trip over her feet. He got there just before she kissed the ground.

"Whoa, sweet girl!" Zaire brought China safely into his arms, holding her close. "I need to teach you to be more mindful of this Texas heat before you seriously hurt yourself. This sun can get hot as hell. Are you feeling okay?"

"Yep," she said, smiling lopsidedly. "It was the surprise that did it, Zaire."

Feeling his tension easing a bit, Zaire cracked up. "I see.

Can I interest you in a bite to eat and a cold drink to help cool you off?"

"The cold drink sounds like a winner. Food, on the other hand, might not be such a good idea." She turned her hand back and forth to relay how unsettled her stomach felt.

"I got it." He pointed at the bicycle rack. "I rode my bike. Come on. I can give you a lift to the dining hall on the handle bars. Or you can sit in back of me."

Recalling how she'd felt seated in front of him astride Thunder, China smiled, allowing her wicked thoughts to run rampant. Had his manhood been affected as much as her libido had reacted to him on that day?

Bernice rushed over to the table as soon as she spotted her son and China seated at a window seat. She loved seeing them together. China had gotten to Zaire and she knew it. She couldn't help hoping this young woman would be exactly what he needed.

Zaire looked at China and smiled. "She had a dizzy spell."

"Poor baby," she cooed. "I have just the remedy if you're nauseous."

"Something cool to drink may be all I can stomach."

"Let me work my magic." She turned to Zaire. "What do you want to order, son?"

Zaire stole a sympathetic glance at China. "Maybe it's not a good idea to eat in front of her. I'll get something later."

Bernice gave her proud approval by planting kisses on both her son's and China's foreheads before leaving.

Zaire tenderly stroked the back of China's hand. "How're you feeling now?"

China managed a believable smile. "Not all the way there, but I feel better. Thanks for rescuing me again."

Zaire grinned. "I kind of like being your rescuer. Please, just don't get into anything too deep for me to handle. I want to continue coming off as your hero."

Knowing for sure Zaire was the sort of hero she'd often dreamed of, China blew him a kiss. "You are so kind. I don't know any man who'd have sympathy pains enough not to want to eat in front of me. That's special."

Zaire shrugged. "As special as you are, I reckon. Mom will fix you up. Don't worry. The lady has a remedy for everything."

Followed by a male waiter carrying a tray, Bernice returned to her son's table. She pointed at a bowl of clear soup. "Set that in front of the lady, please, Eric." Bernice then removed from the tray a platter of light crackers and a serving dish of thinly sliced cheeses. "The key is to eat slowly, China. Take in a little bit of food at a time. The soup and crackers should soothe your stomach so you can eat a decent meal later on. First, drink this." She revealed a fizzy drink that looked a lot like seltzer.

China hid her skepticism. This wonderful woman had gone above and beyond the call of duty to try and help her. She wouldn't think of showing an ounce of ingratitude.

Zaire had no idea how his mother had kept out of sight the brown bag she'd directly placed in his lap, but she had. Inside the bag, he knew she'd packed his favorite turkey club sandwich, a garden salad and two small containers of dressing, a fat dill pickle and a bag of cheese curls. It was his norm.

Surprisingly, China felt much better. She had drunk the seltzer water first. Just as Bernice had instructed, she'd eaten slowly. The soup had been nothing more than a light chicken broth, but it hadn't been salty. She'd eaten a few slices of white cheese, without any negative results. Bernice did know her remedies.

Even though the air was muggy and hot, China loved being on Zaire's bicycle, riding to her cabin. He had offered to get a vehicle to give her a lift in but she'd opted for the bike instead, loving the intimacy riding double afforded them.

The couple dismounted the bicycle, and Zaire walked her to the cabin door. "Need help getting settled in?"

China smiled wryly. "I don't, but I'd like you to come in if you have a moment." She looked at him through hopeful eyes.

"I'd love to come in for a few minutes. I've got a couple of things coming up, but nothing immediate." Standing back, he waited for her to open the door, following right behind her as she entered.

"Make yourself comfortable, Zaire. I'll be right back." She wanted to brush her teeth and freshen up a bit.

"Take your time, China. I'll be here." He walked over to the sofa and sat down.

Zaire couldn't help smiling. He'd run into countless female guests out here on the ranch, but he'd never shared any one-on-one time with a single lady. There were many women who'd tried to lure him back to their accommodations for a chat or a nightcap, but he'd never given in to demands to share his personal time.

The women were attractive enough and as sexy as they came, but that was the extent of it for him. He'd never felt any spiritual or emotional connection with any female guest before now. Since he didn't know where this venture was heading, it scared and concerned him, because he truly loved each and every moment he'd spent with China.

Outside of the one heated exchange between them, Zaire had no cause to entertain regret. What was most surprising to him was how he constantly found himself looking forward to the next time he'd be in her refreshing company.

China popped back into the room. She went over to the sofa and sat down next to Zaire.

"Feeling better?"

"I am. Ms. Bernice is a lifesaver. Once you leave, I plan to lie down until it's time for the evening event. I'm on vacation. When I return home, I have two more days to rest. Then I have my first twelve-hour shift. I usually work from seven in the morning to seven at night."

Zaire frowned. "What's up with the twelve-hour shifts?"

China shrugged. "Most hospitals operate on the same type of schedule these days. It's really not that bad. We're so busy all the time, the shifts go really fast. However, you seem to work longer hours than I do. Why's it okay for you and not for me?"

Shaking his head from side to side, Zaire laughed. "I never said it wasn't okay for you. I was merely satisfying my curiosity. I'm wondering how effective someone can be at such a critical job when working that many hours straight."

"Trust me, we are extremely effective. We can't afford not to be. Sure, there are probably bad nurses, but for the most part we are very dedicated. Lives are at stake and I'd never risk a patient's life by not getting enough rest before going to work. That's called negligence."

"You've made several great points." Zaire got to his feet. "Come on, China. Walk me to the door so you can get settled into bed. I want you to get plenty of rest. You might want to stay out late this evening. The fireworks don't go off until late."

China stood and instantly slipped her hand into Zaire's. "I'm looking forward to more fireworks." She wiggled her eyebrows suggestively. "I like the idea of a bonfire. Do all your women come to events on the ranch?"

China hated the stupid remark as soon as she heard it play back in her ears. Zaire looked as though he'd been slapped across the face. She had offended him. "I'm sorry. I shouldn't have said that."

Zaire gently squeezed her fingers. "No, you shouldn't have. But maybe you want to tell me why a statement like that was floating around in your head."

Continuing the few steps over to the door, China leaned against the doorjamb. "I don't know where it came from. It was a really immature remark."

"It came from your brain. For whatever reason, you must believe I have a long list of women I entertain. Is that true?"

"No it isn't. It was a stupid, spontaneous remark, nothing more."

Zaire had to laugh. "You're full of it, you know."

China laughed. "I'm that, too. My answer can't change because I don't know why I said it."

"I think you *do,* but let me set the record straight. Contrary to your thoughts, I don't have a string of ladies at my beck and call. In fact, I can't think of a single one I can call right off the top of my head. Let me put it like this. I'm not looking for one-night stands or one affair right after another. My rancher lifestyle isn't very appetizing to many women, yet some say they can get used to it. For your information, you're the first woman I've gotten this close to in a long time."

China's heart was cheering up a storm. Zaire had just bared his soul to her and she believed every word he'd said. No matter what happened in the future, they had right now…and that was enough for her. "Say no more. I've been set straight. Thank you."

Nuzzling her neck with his nose, Zaire inhaled China's

exotic scent. "You always smell so good. Turning her face toward his, he looked into her eyes hoping he was rightly reading the contentment he saw there. He felt as satisfied as she looked. Lowering his head, he claimed the most delicious-looking lips he'd ever seen or tasted.

Hungry for the taste of his mouth, China kissed Zaire back, devouring his lips like candy. Latent heat shot through to the depths of her skin, engulfing her entire body. She was too far into the moment to care. Neither one had a crystal ball, but they had each other for however long it lasted. China was content with that.

Zaire kept his eyes shut. Imagining China stripped down to black panties and a seductive black bra had his manhood hard and ready to be inside her. Vowing to not lose control, he did his best to keep a grip.

Totally losing himself in China's kiss, Zaire's mind battled with right and wrong. If they somehow ended up making love, he knew it would turn his world upside down. China had already had a profound effect on his emotions, but making love to her would cause them to soar into the heavens.

The beautiful ballad "I Believe in You and Me" suddenly waltzed into his head. No one would ever know how much he wished he had a woman to believe in and to have her believe in him in return.

Embracing each side of Zaire's face with gentle hands, China had a hard time containing her desire to have all of him. His baby-soft skin melted against her fingers, and her intimate zones were fired up.

In one gentle motion, Zaire pushed China slightly away from him, though he liked how snugly she fit against his body. His eyes locked with hers in a tender embrace. Wishing his heartbeat would slow, he sighed. Lacing his fingers together with hers, he held them up for a brief moment. He looked into her eyes. "Do you trust me?"

Puzzled by his query, China slightly frowned. "Can you expound on that?"

Zaire's eyes narrowed. "The question I asked doesn't need further explanation. Do you trust me? Do you know what it means?"

"Of course I know. To believe in or rely upon, et cetera, et cetera. I believe in you, and I know I can rely on you. So, yes, I'd have to say I trust you." China paused. "Is my trust misplaced? Are you trustworthy, Zaire?"

"I'm very trustworthy, China. You can trust me."

China smiled softly. "We've managed to set each other straight this time." Kissing her thumb, she tenderly pressed it against his lower lip. "Here's to trust, Zaire, between you and me."

He brought his head down until her lips met with his. Kissing her passionately excited him to no end. Her mouth was moist and supple, and she smelled so sweet. His senses had heightened unbelievably, causing his heart to pound like a jackhammer. Zaire had never desired a woman the way he wanted China.

Zaire steered China over to the sofa, where he sat and pulled her down onto his lap. Locking his hands into her hair, kissing her deeply, repeatedly, he felt like he was on top of the world. His manhood was unyieldingly hard.

Shutting down his thoughts, Zaire continued his seduction of the woman his mind and body would burn for day and night. Daring to reach under her shirt and touch the naked flesh between her breast and panties, it felt as if his fingers had caught on fire.

China wanted Zaire, wanted him more than she had any right to. All those dreams of him inside her could become a stark reality, right here, right now.

Was that wise? Would Zaire think she was easy? Well, if he keeps up this fiery manipulation, I won't know the out-come until after he makes me his. Am I truly prepared to take whatever he has to offer and to give whatever he ex-pects of me?

Chapter 7

Morgan strummed his guitar while Bernice softly sang a camp song. Listening intently to the song's lyrics, everyone seated around the blazing campfire appeared comfortable and cozy. Many eyes reflected embers of glowing firelight. Families were grouped together, holding hands, appearing happy. The Kingdom family was no exception. Their hands weren't joined, but the periodic locking of love-filled eyes spoke of internal joys and memorable moments still to come.

"Does everyone know 'God Bless America'?" Morgan asked.

Positive shouts, cheers and whistles filled the air.

"It sounds like everyone's in. Let's all sing it together," Bernice suggested, leading in the song as everyone joined it.

China continuously stole covert glances at Zaire as he sang along with the others. She'd never seen a person who fit so perfectly into his surroundings. Texas ranching was made for him, and he was made for Western-style living. It seemed like such a simple life to her, possibly even a stress-free existence. He'd explained a lot about his life to her earlier.

Zaire's existence certainly was busy, but it was a far cry from the hectic world she moved in. There were times when she was so tired she'd just barely drag herself off to bed. She couldn't begin to count the evenings after work she'd come into the house only to immediately drop down onto the sofa, staying there until the wee hours of the morning.

"When are we going to eat?" one young boy childishly whined. "I want some hot dogs, soda pop and chips."

The entire group laughed at his animated remarks.

Glancing over at his wife, Morgan carefully laid aside the guitar. Bernice instantly whipped into action to get the meal served. After gathering together all the youngsters, she handed out long-handled hot dog skewers.

China easily recalled when she and her friends had used wire coat hangers to cook hot dogs and marshmallows when wiener roasts were held in local parks at home. She watched attentively as adults helped younger children skewer hot dogs for roasting over the open fire. Dads were great with sons, and mothers paid special attention to their daughters. Big brothers and sisters appeared to relish helping out the younger siblings.

The bonfire event was indeed a family affair. Laughter rang out all over the place. If someone burned a marshmallow to a crisp or blackened a hot dog, the laughter grew even louder. Surprisingly enough, no taunting occurred.

Over an hour had passed before Morgan was back to strumming his guitar and Bernice had begun singing songs again, entertaining the large number of guests. Everyone began to sing along with the music, clapping in tune to the spirited CW flavor.

When they began to perform one of Zaire's favorite songs, he rushed over to claim the lady he could hardly wait to dance with. Taking her by the hand, he steered China to the designated dance area.

"Are you familiar with the 'Cotton-Eyed Joe'?" Zaire asked China.

She frowned. "The folk song?"

"The line dance, China. It was performed in the 1980 movie *Urban Cowboy.*"

"Dad had that movie on VHS, but I can't remember it that well."

"The steps are called out in this dance, so just follow my lead. It might take you a minute to catch on."

China laughed. "I'm sure it'll take way more than a minute."

As soon as Zaire started the popular line dance, other guests hustled over to the dancing area highlighted by a bright spotlight. With his arm firmly around China's waist, Zaire began talking her through the lively steps.

China loved the tender feel of Zaire's hands on her waistline, feeling his heat right through her denim dress. Normally she'd be embarrassed by making so many missteps, but Zaire kept whispering to her to simply go with his flow and have fun.

It took China longer than she had anticipated to get the steps right, but she loved the patience of the man instructing her.

Laughing, without any inhibition whatsoever and flirtatiously swaying her body, China paced her steps under the tutelage of the sexiest man present. Zaire had great dance moves, stepping smoothly, easily. She couldn't wait for the music to slow down. Feeling her soft body meshed against his hard form was a moment she eagerly awaited.

As China thought back on how they'd fallen asleep on the sofa earlier, she couldn't keep from smiling. She didn't know exactly when Zaire had left the cabin. Awakening much later, she was alone with just the scent of his cologne. They hadn't made love. He deserved all the credit for not allowing them to do something they might come to regret. He had decided it was best not to rush things. China had agreed.

Zaire was a very private man, one who didn't particularly like to indulge in public displays of affection, but it was hard for him to resist kissing China breathless. She had the kind of full, ripe lips that drove him crazy. "You'd better stop leading me into temptation." Grinning wickedly, his eyes held a delectable warning of heated danger.

China laughed flirtatiously. "Are you asking me to deliver you from evil? If so, you'll have to consult a higher power. The bad girl in me can only lead you astray."

The music slowed. Pulling China nearer to his body, Zaire pressed his hand against the back of her head, drawing it to him. "Lead me there, sweetheart. I'm not a follower, but I'll be right behind you, wherever you go. Just know that I'll always keep you safe."

China was moved. "In that case, let's hit one of your favorite haunts on the ranch. I'm sure you have a special place where you witness the beauty of nightfall."

"I have a few places I love to visit after dark. We'll have to go on horseback. Are you up to riding?"

Looking apprehensive, China nodded. "I…think…so."

Zaire chuckled at her stammering. "You can ride Thunder with me. Deal?"

Lifting her hand, she slapped it against his palm. "Deal!"

"Stay with my family until I return. I'll drive the SUV

down to the stables and saddle up Thunder. We'll be back in less than a half hour."

China nodded, nervously shuffling her feet. "I think I want to try and ride on my own. Pick out the tamest horse. Don't you think I should just go with you now? Managing two horses at one time sounds dangerous."

Zaire chuckled. "I know why it'd seem that way to you. It's nothing for me to control several horses. But I like your suggestion." He reached for her hand. "Let's go."

China looked over to where Zaire's family was gathered. "Aren't you telling anyone we're leaving?"

"They'll find out soon enough. I can promise you that. We'll be well on our way to Lookout Point before they realize we're missing in action."

China laughed. "You are too crazy." Sliding her hand into his, she smiled brightly. "Making another memory with you will be pleasurable. I just know it."

"That makes two of us."

As the two horses trotted along side by side, China was so proud of the courage she'd shown by riding solo. Knowing she'd be terrified if the horses went any faster, Zaire set a pace that was quite suitable for her beginning-rider status.

Reaching down with her free hand, China gently stroked the small horse's white mane. The caress only lasted a few seconds. Holding both reins tightly in her hand made her feel safer. Zaire had referred to Bluebonnet as a pony, saying the kids loved to ride her. The horse's name fit her startling blue eyes—and it was the name of Texas's state flower.

China wasn't a kid but she felt like one, loving the gentle way the animal performed for her. The steady trotting and clop-clop sounds of the horseshoes hitting the ground was actually soothing. China felt tranquil.

Marveling at the majestic surroundings, she sighed with deep reverence. The dark sky was streaked with an array of pastel shades and a host of grayish clouds. The moon appeared to stand guard over the universe. Giant cacti appeared to take on lives of their own. A melodic chorus of nightfall sounds induced peace.

While peering over at China, Zaire was happy her eyes held no fear. Still, the rigid way she sat atop the horse made him wonder if she was angst ridden. He sidled Thunder closer to Bluebonnet. "How're you feeling?"

"Exhilarated! I'm steadily making peace with Bluebonnet. She's been superb."

"Glad to hear it, China. As you get used to her you'll relax even more."

Fully stretched out on the blanket Zaire had spread beneath the massive tree at Lookout Point, the couple held each other close, their heads sharing one pillow. If not for the sweet melodies coming from the foraging creatures of the night, total silence would engulf them. Zaire had many favorite spots on the ranch, but this one was a headliner.

He'd never shared this special place with anyone outside his family circle. So much had changed for him since meeting China…and so fast.

Having China lying right next to him, her leg thrown loosely over his hip, made this encounter seem so surreal. Despite the fact that she had on a short white button-down denim dress, she hadn't let it interfere in how she'd placed her leg.

Zaire tried desperately to curb his R-rated thoughts, but each attempt was unsuccessful. She was so close to him. Such easy access to her precious treasure, he thought, tenderly stroking her bare leg. Wickedly intimate images rushed headlong through his mind, wreaking havoc on what little composure he had left.

Desiring to satisfy his need for her, Zaire turned his head and captured China's lips with his own. Her fiery response had him floating. Kissing her again and again helped satisfy his need for the taste of her mouth. But he had other needs, manly ones.

To distract himself, Zaire looked up at the sky for several seconds. Smiling softly, he pointed toward the heavens. "There's the Big Dipper. Can you make it out?"

China followed the direction of Zaire's gaze. "Yeah, I can. Dad showed me how to locate constellations when I was eight or nine. It took me a long time to make out each one, but I eventually got good at it."

"It's no easy task, especially when a person lives in the city, where stars like this just don't get a chance to shine. Smog often hides the sky's beautiful lightshows."

"I know. That's why Dad liked the open range so much. He used to tell me how stars shone so brightly at night out here. He loved his Texas. That's for sure. Just as much as I love my city of L.A. There's never a dull moment in that place, and the nightlife is unbelievably exciting."

Bending his head, Zaire feathered kisses onto China's cheeks, moving down to her lower lip. His taunting tongue teased her mouth until she opened up for it to enter. The next several kisses were light and playful.

As the kiss grew hotter with passion, China found it hard to keep from squirming. Her body was on fire from Zaire's burning touch. They'd come so close to making love earlier, but it hadn't happened. China was having mixed emotions about their decision.

Lying flat on his back, Zaire rolled China over until she was on top of him. Wrapping her up in his arms, he kissed her passionately. Slightly loosening his grip on her, his hand roved the back of her thighs with tenderness.

Prompted by his nearly out-of-control desire, Zaire took his explorations further, slipping his hand under China's dress and caressing her silk-clad rear. Feeling the prickly heat of her flesh through her panties, his one desperate desire was to cool down her body—and heat it right back up, over and over again.

China moaned softly, gulping down his kisses, enjoying the sweet flavor of his plundering tongue. As if his kiss was her favorite soft drink, she didn't want the satisfaction to end. Moving her hands over his head, she moaned from sheer pleasure. As his hands reached inside her panties, she stiffened for a brief moment. Growing totally relaxed, she ground her hips against his. His hands burned her flesh with the heat of passion, making her feel indescribable fires of steadily mounting desires.

Zaire kissed China's ear. "I have a confession. I don't think I could've stopped us earlier if I'd had a condom. I wouldn't have wanted to stop."

At the moment, he didn't have a lot of control over his body, but he had protection. Still, he wasn't prepared to let things get out of control. China had to be the one to give the go-ahead.

China rolled off Zaire, turned on her side and looked down into his eyes. She saw deep desire for her there. "Thanks for being honest." He wanted her as much as she wanted him. Her hand went for the shiny silver buckle on his belt.

China's confidence began to soar when her fingers didn't tremble at all and Zaire wasn't pushing away her hand. Believing they were on the same page, keeping her gaze locked into his, she loosened the buckle and slowly tugged off the belt. Lowering her head, she kissed him full on the mouth. Kissing him fervently, taking hold of his zipper, she pulled it down.

Zaire lifted his hips. "Take my jeans off if you want me."

China's eyes twinkled with mischief. "If you think I want you, take them off for me."

Chuckling lowly, Zaire shoved at the jeans until they rested down around his ankles. "If you finish what I started, I'll know we're in this together."

Being on the same page as Zaire only heightened the thrill of it all. Without uttering a word, China slipped the jeans over his feet and tossed them aside.

As much as Zaire wanted to completely disrobe China, he'd also come to the conclusion that it'd be exciting to make love to her with her clothes on. There was something hot and delectable about pushing up China's dress for the sole purpose of gaining access to her intimate zone.

He rolled halfway on top of China. Looking down into her blazing eyes, reaching under her dress, he lazily parted the panties from her body. Lowering his head, he tenderly caressed the outer areas of her womanhood and made China squirm uncontrollably.

From what Zaire observed, all systems were on green. The anticipation alone was enough to do him in, but he wouldn't dare give in to defeat. Using his thumb, he massaged the lips of her soft, moist womanhood. Inserting one finger gently inside her, then another, he tenderly stroked her inner core.

Rolling up on his side, he looked down into her face. "No matter what happens with us, days of uncertainty are ahead of us. I hate thinking of you leaving the ranch. I feel dreadful every time it's brought up."

China rested the back of her hand against Zaire's left cheek. "Let's not think about it then. We both know it's inevitable. Our end result is already destined. I believe that, Zaire."

"I believe it, too. Let's make every single moment special."

China was too hot to turn back now. Taking the condom from his hand, she tore it open and handed it back to him. As she watched him roll on the protection, the act itself made her feverish.

Once the condom was in place, China finished taking off his white boxers. Straddling Zaire's body, she felt her moist flesh was ready to slowly open around his fully-erect manhood. She had no idea how he liked to be pleasured, but she'd find out.

Eyes wide with astonishment, feeling a tad hesitant and uncertain, Zaire licked his dry lips, hungry for China's exotic flavoring. His eyes were fastened on her when a muffled yet mystified groan suddenly escaped her throat.

Shutting her eyes, China lowered her body down onto his thickened organ. Moaning softly, her teeth clenched her lower lip until waves of desire completely engulfed her. Tossing her head back, locking her fingers firmly behind his head, she drew him deeper inside of her.

China opened her eyes and looked directly at him.

Zaire saw passion shimmering in her eyes. Her next passionate moan pierced his ears.

China continued to slowly move atop him, grinding her hips into his, reveling in the delicious sensations, concentrating solely on the unrelenting pleasure cruising through her intimate zone. Having Zaire inside her captured the moment she'd been dreaming about. Since the first second she'd realized her wild attraction to him, her thoughts had included wildly sexual fantasies.

If China lived to be a hundred, she was positive she'd never regret making passionate love to Zaire Kingdom.

Working their bodies into a wild frenzy made her feel ecstatic. Everything was so good, so right for her.

No turning back for them now, Zaire thought. They were joined as one, in the flesh, and he wanted more. Awakening in him sensation after sensation, his mind went blank.

Zaire groaned, gently driving his manhood deeper and deeper. "You are so beautiful, China. Amazing."

Raising her head to bring their mouths together, China sweetly silenced Zaire, kissing him passionately.

Together, they created a beautiful symphony out of warm, tender lovemaking. The fiery friction sparking between them was surreal, yet very real.

China's hips responded as Zaire ground his hips and manhood into her with a tender force. Feeling as though she'd been catapulted into the sky, the rocking back and forth had her matching his fervor stroke for stroke. She couldn't get enough of Zaire—and he never wanted the hot, sweet torturing of his body to end.

Trembling within, China knew Zaire was close to blowing the lid off her libido and her sanity. Moving with wild abandon, taking in all of him, she dug her fingernails into his back, purring with pleasure. Her body tensed up briefly then went completely lax. The earth felt as if it was moving, turning her world around in circles. "Take me…all the way…home, Zaire," she cried huskily.

Zaire claimed her mouth in another wet, passionate kiss. "We're going home together," he whispered in return. "Don't hold back. Let go. Remember I promised to follow wherever you lead."

"I remem…" Her body shaking uncontrollably cut off a response. "I'm home," she cried shakily. "I want to stay right here."

Feeling his body uniting with hers on the road to paradise, Zaire unleashed a fury of tender plunges and electrifying grinds until his heat spilled inside her, leaving him shaking, weak and utterly satisfied.

Zaire pulled China into his arms. "I am overwhelmed."

"Me, too," she said, wishing she could feel this alive every waking moment. Every nerve in her body felt exposed, and the nonstop tingling felt sensational.

Reaching down for the blanket, Zaire pulled it up over them, moving his hand around until he found the pillow. Slightly lifting his head, he lodged the pillow beneath it then made sure her head was positioned comfortably. "You are amazing. I feel incredible, China. Making love to you has fulfilled my constant desire."

China sighed with contentment. "Same here. I've thought about us coming together like this so many times. It was so much more than I'd imagined."

"You can say that again. Reality far surpassed my fiery dreams. What now?"

It didn't take Zaire long to realize why China hadn't answered him. She was fast asleep. He was a little disappointed in her checking out on him, but only because he had hoped they'd share their true feelings about what had just occurred. She had given herself to him and he wanted to let her know he'd always cherish it.

It took Zaire even less time to realize he was acting stupidly. China was more than likely asleep because she had been fully satisfied and felt total contentment. As he thought of how wildly her body had responded to his, he smiled, closing his eyes. Tightening his hold on her, he basked in the engulfing peace.

Zaire awakened just minutes before sunrise. With China nowhere to be seen, he became alarmed. He saw her clothing piled in a heap on the blanket. Wherever she was, she was naked. As the sounds of splashing water suddenly reached his ears, he threw his head back and laughed. Jumping up from the ground, he zipped down to the lake just a few yards away.

Without hesitation Zaire dove into the warm waters heading straight for China. Although she had seen him enter the lake, he hadn't surfaced yet. She howled as his arms wrapped around her legs. Finally coming up for air, he gulped in a few fresh breaths. Pulling her into his arms, he kissed her breathless. Then they basked in the sunrise.

China pulled her head back. "Missed me, huh?"

"Like crazy," he responded.

Meshing her mouth hungrily against Zaire's, China kissed him passionately, her tongue coiling around his. Placing her hands on both sides of his face, she looked into his eyes. "I'm glad you're here, happy you heard the water." She lowered her lashes for a moment. "Can we make love again, right here in the lake?"

"You didn't have to ask." Lifting her into his arms, he wrapped her legs around his waist. "I want to make love to you in all my special places on the ranch."

China laughed. "I can hardly wait, Zaire. Can we make love in a hayloft, using a bed of hay to lie on?"

"Just so happens that the barns are one of my favorite places to go when I want to disappear. I've fallen asleep in one many a night. I don't go there with the intent to stay. I'm usually so tired it ends up that way. I love the smell of freshly pitched hay. It's as powerful as taking a sleeping pill."

China nodded. "Hmm, sounds divine. I'll be counting down the hours."

"You're serious about the barn, aren't you?"

"What makes you think I wasn't? Of course I am!"

Zaire laughed. "You completely bowl me over."

Turning his back to her, he tore open the condom packet

he held. Getting it situated in the water was challenging, but his hands were adept. Condom secure, he turned and reached for China, guiding her hand to his hardened length.

Feeling the latex covering his manhood, China smiled. Wrapping one of her legs up around his waist, she pulled down his head, kissing him hungrily. Moaning softly as Zaire came into her, she closed her eyes to savor the delicious feel of his manhood.

Zaire tantalized China with a slow technique of lovemaking, wanting to take his time in pleasuring her to the fullest. Hoisting her up into his arms, he waited until both her legs were around him.

The first upward thrust caused China to toss her head back. Holding on tightly to him, she drew his thrusts deeper inside. Water lapped about, but each was only aware of white-hot fires and crazy desire cruising through their bodies.

Moving farther out into the water, Zaire kept their bodies locked together. Using aggressively sexy moves, China moved up and down his manhood vigorously, loving the spiking friction. Hands gently touched and tenderly caressed. Lips kissed and tongues wildly teased highly sensitive nipples. The beginning of a climax rushed through her and she moved up and down on him faster. Seconds later, an explosion detonated inside them.

An hour had passed when a moment of sadness suddenly gripped Zaire. Fully dressed, lying on the blanket, he looked up at the sky. He temporarily warded off thoughts of China leaving, knowing he'd have to deal with it sooner or later. Her departure often loomed over him like a dark thunder cloud, yet he had so much to be happy about.

Zaire hated thinking about time, but he had to. "We'd

better get back. I have a riding class in an hour. Are you signed up?"

"I'm not, but can I come to class anyway? Riding Blue-bonnet felt really good. She's so tame. Can I train on her for the rest of my stay?"

Knowing her every wish was his command, Zaire grinned. "You can join us. Bluebonnet is yours exclusively. I won't let anyone else ride her. I'll tell Morgan, Zurich and Zane." He crossed his heart. "You have my word, China."

China kissed Zaire full on the mouth. "Our deal is sealed."

Zaire grinned. "I like the way you close a deal."

China smiled brightly. "Closing one with you is sweet. If you're ready to go, I'll race you back to the tree. If I win, you have to sing one of my favorite songs. 'Tie a Yellow Ribbon 'Round the Ole Oak Tree.'"

"Tony Orlando, huh? You went way back in our parents' day on that one. And I *do* know the words to it, every last one."

Clapping her hands, China laughed. "We'll find out, won't we?" With that said, and no warning, she jumped up and took off running.

China's sexy body had Zaire spellbound, his mouth agape. He watched after her for several seconds before whipping into action, overtaking her easily. Wishing he'd chosen some type of consequence for the loser, he turned around and ran backward. China's strides were hopeless against his much longer ones. "You're the loser. What're you going to do for me?" he asked. "You never had a chance of winning."

"Since you didn't put any conditions on me beforehand, I get off scot-free."

"That's what you think. You lost, China, so you have to pay. You'd better believe the payment will be a good one."

* * *

Instead of showering, China filled the tub with steaming hot water, agitating the strawberry bubble bath she'd poured in. Getting into the tub, she instantly found her comfort zone. Laying her head back on the bath pillow, her mind drifted back to the night and morning spent with Zaire.

A smile formed on her mouth and her eyes lit up at the same time. Never before had she slept outdoors all night. She'd had plenty of sleepovers with her friends when younger, but never outside.

As it often did, China's mind turned to her departure. She couldn't help wondering if it had been foolish of her to have gotten this involved with Zaire. It was too late now. She was more than involved, she quietly admitted.

China was in love. As sure as she was breathing, she had fallen madly in love with Zaire Kingdom. Nothing compared to the feelings she experienced when they were together. They still had several days to build more awesome memories.

Leaving Whispering Lakes Ranch was one thing. Getting Zaire out of her head and evicting him from her heart was another matter entirely. China didn't think she'd ever get over her deep feelings for him. Furthermore, she didn't want to. Distance was definitely a major issue for them, but true love had a way of winning out over serious obstacles. If he loved her the way she loved him, they could make it. But no mention of love had been made by either one.

Did Zaire love her? Had he fallen just as hard for her as she had for him?

At this moment, China could only wonder.

Chapter 8

Glad she'd worn long jeans instead of shorts, China sat in the saddle atop Bluebonnet. So far, all they'd done was trot around the ring. Zaire was working with several other guests, mainly young children. It was amazing for China to see how great he was with kids, explaining every little detail.

"Most important thing is for each of you to get to know your mount. Make friends with him or her." Zaire had told the children each horse's name. Smaller kids seemed animated; teenagers appeared a little less than enthused.

"Horses love to be petted and pampered, but keep your hands clear of their mouths. I'll show you how to feed them treats after class. When dismounted, stand near the middle of the horse. You don't want to be in front of or behind it. A swift kick can result in major injuries. Now follow my lead. Do only what I instruct you to."

Zaire slowly trotted Thunder around the ring, making

sure to keep a strong yet relaxed grip on the reins. "Talk softly to your horse as you guide it, telling it what you want it to do," he instructed. "Each animal knows its name. Go around the ring again so I can observe. Keep moving and stay a good distance from your neighbor."

Keeping watchful eyes on the class, keenly alert, Zaire smiled when things went well, frowning when displeased. "Don't lean too far forward. You can easily stroke your mount without getting into an uncomfortable position. A horse's mane is long, and your steed can feel your hands."

For the next forty-five minutes Zaire imparted a mere fraction of his vast knowledge on the art of riding a horse. China found herself hanging on his every word. From the looks of things, he had earned the rapt attention of everyone present. He was a highly intelligent man and a very accomplished one. She knew she could learn a lot from him. In fact, she'd already learned so much.

China felt like turning away when Zaire came toward her. She hoped he hadn't caught her watching him so intently. It had been hard to keep her eyes off him. Watching him brought her so much pleasure.

Thunder circled Bluebonnet under Zaire's direction. It seemed to China that the male horse was actually flirting. Thunder briefly rested his head on her horse's neck as though giving the lady a hug. China's eyes leveled on Zaire when he began laughing, amused by Thunder's amorous advances.

"Is that something you taught Thunder?" China asked. "He's kind of frisky."

"He's a big stud. Thunder loves the ladies. Bluebonnet enjoyed his attention."

"How do you know?"

"She would've protested loudly if she hadn't. A few

warning snorts would've sent old Thunder on his way. She liked it. Bluebonnet knows how to put up a fuss."

China had to laugh at the idea of Thunder finding Bluebonnet attractive. Well, just like humans, horses hooked up, too, China mused, laughing.

As the class wound down, students trotted their mounts around the ring for a final lap.

"Okay, folks, that's it. I'm proud of you. Everyone did great. For those continuing the class, we'll meet here tomorrow at the same time. You can ride your horse back to the stables or use the reins to lead it. We'll all head out in a few minutes."

It was China's turn to show off her stuff. She felt comfortable and was sure she could do what was expected of her. Handling Bluebonnet like a pro, she strutted the small horse around the ring, proving she had firm command. She beamed at Zaire's smiling approval.

China slowly propelled the horse into a light gallop. Catching up to Zaire, she rode alongside him in silence. She had a good idea where her peace and contentment came from. The land welcomed her. Bluebonnet tolerated her. And Zaire and his family made her feel like she belonged there.

At this moment in time, I do belong here.

Always the patient instructor, Zaire was still in teaching mode inside the barn.

"Carefully remove your horse's saddle and hang it up. The name of each horse is etched on a wood plank. Once you've settled your mount, class is dismissed. Enjoy the rest of your day."

Zaire again told his class what a great job they'd done. Once all horses were put away, he bade the students a good afternoon.

* * *

Seated with Zaire at a table in the dining room, China had a turkey sandwich in front of her, a small garden salad and a tall glass of raspberry iced tea. He munched on a chicken salad sandwich on a kaiser roll. He had a chef's salad but the same cold drink as his companion.

Zaire looked around the room for his mother. It was unusual for her not to have shown her face by now. He and China had been there for about thirty minutes. Spotting his aunts entering the dining room, Zaire summoned them with the wave of his hand. The somber expression on their faces had him worried.

"Hey, nephew," Ethel greeted warmly. "It's nice to see you, China."

"Where's Mom? I haven't seen her since I sat down."

The other sisters acknowledged Zaire and China before sitting down.

Looking nervous, Josephine covered Zaire's hand with hers. "Morgan took her in town to the hospital. There was a small fire in the kitchen, and her hand got burned. I don't know if it's serious, but she was in pain. Thank God Morgan was present."

Zaire shot straight to his feet. "Do Zurich and Zane know?"

"They're following behind Morgan in Zane's truck. Hailey is with them, too."

"Please have a waitress wrap my lunch and store it for me. I'm going into town."

Dorothy collected Zaire's plate and drink. In parting, she kissed her nephew's cheek. "Don't worry. Bernice is a strong sister."

The other two sisters gave their farewells and left with Dorothy.

Zaire turned to China. "Will you be okay while I'm gone? I've got to see about my mother."

Concern glowing in her eyes, China nodded. "Go. I'll be fine." She hesitated. "Is it okay if I come with you? I'd like to be there."

"Sure you can. Thanks for asking. I'd love your company."

China got to her feet. Wrapping her arms around Zaire's waist, she looked up at him. "It'll be okay." With that said, standing on her tiptoes, she kissed both his cheeks, feeling good that she'd asked to ride along. She was only too happy to go with him.

Just as Zaire and China turned to leave, Dorothy was there, thrusting a brown bag containing his uneaten lunch into his hand. The tall foam cups she handed him held fresh cold drinks. "Be careful, Zaire. Obey the speed limits, child."

Chuckling, Zaire tipped his hat. "You know I will, Aunt Dorothy. Thanks for everything." After a warm, loving glance at his aunt, he took off to trade the truck for his SUV, telling China he'd meet her in front in about fifteen minutes.

China turned to Dorothy. "What happened to Ms. Bernice?"

Dorothy shrugged. "I wish I knew. By the time I saw her, Morgan had already wrapped her hand. She told him to get Zaire, but he was hell-bent on taking her to the E.R. She'll be okay. Bernice is the strongest woman in our family."

China sighed. "The burn to her hand could be troublesome. If Ms. Bernice can't cook, she'll go stone crazy."

Dorothy laughed along with China, which made both women feel much better.

Knowing she had to be cautious about what to say or not to say, Dorothy eyed China closely, noticing the special glow shining through when a woman is in love. "You're in love with Zaire, aren't you?"

China widened her eyes. "What makes you say that?"

"You have a glow about you. I didn't see it when you first arrived. You seem so surprised by my question. Why's that?"

Chuckling nervously, China looked down at the floor. "I guess you caught me off guard. So I have a glow, huh? I've noticed it when I look in the mirror. I *am* in love with Zaire. He doesn't know it and I don't want him to."

Smiling softly, Dorothy nodded. "Why don't you want him to know the truth?"

Trying to be aloof, China shrugged. "That's a tough question, same one I've asked myself. The only believable reason I can come up with is that I'm leaving here soon. Long-distance lovers, I don't know if it can work."

Dorothy smiled. "It can if you both work at it."

"Ms. Dorothy, we live so far apart. All we have going for us is right now. I'll have to be content in hanging out with him and going home when it's time. Will I miss him? You bet! How can I not if I love him?"

"Love and sacrifices go hand-in-hand. What about moving here? Now that's what I call a sacrifice, sweetheart."

China instantly paled. "Move here! My life is in L.A. I love the city. It's my home and I'm content there."

"Can't your life be wherever the man you love is? What about it?"

"Where is this coming from?" China threw up her hands. "I said I was in love with Zaire. I haven't heard anyone say he loves me back. A relationship takes two people to work. Here's a question for you. Would Zaire move to L.A. for me?"

Dorothy's eyes softened with compassion. "Talking

about where a life is! This ranch is Zaire's. Everything around here was planned by him. My other nephews have lots of input, but the CEO is Zaire. He's a brilliant architect and he helped build this place with his own two hands. But work without love isn't as rewarding."

China laughed. "Okay, I'd better run before we get any deeper into this. I'm sure Zaire is outside waiting for me. He went to swap out the truck for his SUV."

"I don't know if this means anything or not, China, but I believe Zaire is in love with you, too. I've seen how relaxed he is with you. No one has gotten his undivided attention in a long time. Keep your options open, child. Don't make any hasty decisions. I think you two are hot together."

China had to smile at Dorothy's word choice, remembering the skinny-dipping in the lake. *We are hot for each other.* "I'll keep in mind everything you said. I'm sure Zaire will call as soon as he has news to share." She lifted Dorothy's hand and kissed it. "It's been nice talking to you."

"Same here, China. You're a delightful young woman."

Enjoying some easy-listening music, lying across the bed on her stomach, China pulled a pillow to her and placed it under her chin. Two hours had passed since Zaire had dropped her off. Before they'd gotten on the road, Zurich had called to say they were on the way back. Everything was fine with their mother.

China had silently prayed for Ms. Bernice to have a quick recovery. The burns weren't second or third degree, but she'd needed treatment. Even though her burn wasn't terribly serious, Zaire still worried. He treasured his mother. It was a beautiful sentiment, one she wished she could experience with her own mom.

The letter Camille had left behind had made China feel unwanted and unloved. Before the letter, she had been able to kid herself. But Camille had spelled out in plain English her feelings on being a mother. Becoming a parent had made Camille feel worse instead of better.

Regardless of what Camille Braxton had or hadn't done, China knew she had turned out just fine. Brody had done a great job of raising her.

Rolling over at the sound of her cell phone, China reached over to the nightstand and picked it up. Without bothering to look at the caller ID, she gave a greeting. "Zaire, how's it going? Is your mom feeling any better? Where are you?"

"Slow down, China. Catch your breath. Mom is coming along fine. I'm back at home. Want to meet me in the hayloft of the red barn around seven?"

Feeling exhilarated, China practically skipped through the field of colorful wildflowers. Cool air had swooped in to push out the muggy humidity. Her hair blew in the breeze as she made her way to the red barn, the rendezvous point.

Stopping dead in her tracks, she gasped, watching the orange sun descend, casting its dimming rays over the landscape. The place looked and felt magical. Tall reeds and massive oaks lined the easy-to-follow route. Several large concrete, cinder block and aluminum buildings made good landmarks. Zaire had told her what she'd see on the way. He just hadn't told her how magnificent her journey would be.

Seeing the bright red barn off in the near distance, she smiled. She had arrived. Running the rest of the way, she reached the barn and rushed inside. Bales of hay were stacked everywhere and a green pitchfork was stuck in one of them.

Spotting a ladder that led up to the hayloft, she made her way over to it and carefully made her ascent. At the top, she looked down at the barn, storing the alluring sights in her memory bank. As she began walking, she saw several stalls and wondered about their purpose. Each looked warm and inviting, and lots of loose hay was stored there. It was the perfect place to lie down and wait for Zaire.

Leaning on the post, his foot firmly planted back against it, Zaire couldn't take his eyes off a sleeping China. Glued to her firm rear, his gaze marveled at such a beautiful form outlined in tight black jeans. A matching jean jacket hung from a hook on a nearby post. Her thin summer shirt allowed him a stimulating eyeful of perfectly rounded breasts. A worn navy blue blanket lay near her bare feet.

China was a stunning woman, a sexy lady who'd seized all his desires, physical and otherwise. Her eventual departure was still bothersome to him, but it hadn't stopped him from succumbing to her sweet charms. Nothing could've kept him in check. He just hadn't been able to hold out. He normally knew where and when to draw the line, but he had no willpower against China. She'd also been eager and willing to take him as her lover. That meant a lot to him.

Lying beneath loose piles of hay, China was unaware of Zaire's presence. She had arrived nearly a half hour before the scheduled time just to acquaint herself with the barn. Further exploration of the land had been fun. The long journey from the cabin had made her a little tired.

Watching China sleep made Zaire feel drowsy. The day had been long and dramatic, and he was bone-tired. Dropping down to the wooden floor, Zaire rested his back on the post and pulled off his new cowboy boots.

China stirred slightly. Trying to keep from disturbing her, Zaire sucked in a deep breath and held it. Part of him wanted her to awaken. He had missed her during their short time of separation. They were seeing more and more of each other outside of the ranch activities she participated in. He didn't want their secret rendezvous to end.

The early-morning skinny-dipping session came to mind. Not once had she given him any indication she doubted or regretted their lovemaking. They'd shared several fiery kisses at the cabin door before he'd taken leave.

"Hi," she whispered softly. "How long have you been here?"

Zaire loved the sound of her voice. "Not long. I didn't want to disturb you."

"Why not? We met here to be together. I would've roused you." Turning up on her side, planting her elbow in a mound of hay, she propped her head on her hand.

"Is that so? I would've been elated by your arousal."

China giggled. She patted the ground next to her. "Come lie down. Get comfortable. You've already taken off your boots."

Obeying her command, Zaire grinned. "I had planned to stretch out and doze off for a minute. But watching you sleep intrigued me more."

Scooting across the short distance to China, he stretched out fully, resting his head on a pallet of hay. Without any prompting from him, she laid her head upon his chest.

After lying quietly for several minutes, she looked at Zaire without raising her head. "In view of Ms. Bernice's injuries, is the square dance still on?"

"Unless it rains, but it's not in the forecast. Most of our guests are signed up. I love it when everyone participates in activities. There was a time when people came out here just to get away from other people. We eventually coaxed folks out of the cabins to join the fun events."

Closing her eyes, China puckered her lips and planted a juicy kiss on his mouth. "I've missed you, corporate cowboy. I've seen some of what you do, but I'd love to hear all about your normal workday. I bet it's fascinating."

Tenderly pressing his finger into the center of China's nose, he gazed down into her eyes. "And I'd love to have another kiss, passionate, just like the first one."

Smiling flirtatiously, China batted her lashes. "I can make it happen."

Lowering her mouth onto his, China teasingly tasted Zaire's lower lip. She then kissed his left and right ear. Staring intently into his eyes, her fingertips smoothed his hair back. "You have the most fascinating eyes. And I love your perfectly-formed mouth. It's thick, juicy and fruity."

Their laughter rang out. Desiring to fulfill Zaire's request, China kissed him passionately, delivering it exactly the way he'd requested.

Trying desperately to lasso his untamed desire for China, Zaire kissed her back, leveling her with raw passion. "You're intrigued with my eyes and mouth. And I'm downright awestruck by every part of you. You are an enchantress." Wondering how he'd get through the rest of his life without her, Zaire briefly considered what hovered between them. It was robust and sizzling.

Rolling over on top of China, Zaire covered her body with his. Pushing his hands through her hair, he rained kisses over her neck and into her hair. Making contact with her sweet, sexy body, his manhood stiffened. "Ever get the feeling we're in trouble?" Zaire asked.

"Deep trouble, Zaire. And I don't mind," said China.

She wrapped her mouth up with his, kissing him deeply. "Mmm, so sweet." Turned on by the way his tongue had slowly captured hers, she felt her body trembling. Melting into him mentally and physically, making hot love to Zaire was all she could think about.

Did she dare go farther? Was she too eager in wanting him?

Unbuckling his belt in haste was the answer to her questions. As China's fingers hovered near his zipper she was close to losing it. If she didn't stop right now, she wouldn't. Knowing how he made her feel, she didn't want to stop. Her mind made up, she slid the crisp jeans over his hips, enjoying the pleasurable unveiling.

With steady hands, China unbuttoned Zaire's shirt, pushing the denim aside. Her hands tenderly roved his broad chest, loving the silky feel of his thick chest hairs. Unable to keep her eyes off his lower body, her gaze followed the continuous trail of hair. Raising her head, she zeroed back in on his chest. His nipples, dark and hard, caused her to gasp. Dying to taste each perfect circle, she licked her lips in anticipation.

Now that Zaire was stripped down to his boxers, China felt like her own clothes had caught fire. Shedding her attire as quickly as possible might keep her body from incinerating. *Too late.* China was already consumed by desire.

Needing Zaire, China lay back in the hay and undid her buttons. Growing impatient with her fumbling fingers, she sighed in frustration. Instead of totally removing her top, she slid it off her shoulders. Lifting her hips, she removed her jeans. Her black panties and bra went next.

Making love to her again was what Zaire had dreamed about the entire day. He couldn't even recall the last time he'd lain in bed with a woman before his first time making love to China. Zaire wasn't into comparing women. Even if he were, there was no comparison to her.

Looking over at his pants, he pondered the difficulties that distance would bring for them. Grabbing his jeans, he removed a condom from his wallet.

Zaire put on protection and moved back to China. This

woman had him lost in a state of reckless wantonness. Pure desire flashed in her eyes. Their bodies uniting in a session of unruliness would produce scrumptious sensations.

By the way her body possessed his, he was sure she was already upon the point of no return. She undoubtedly wanted him, all of him. And he wanted every inch of her, urgently so.

Zaire felt sweetly agonizing pleasure which far outweighed any measure of guilt. Pulling her up his body until her nipples grazed his chest, Zaire wrapped his arms around her. "You are one naughty girl. This tame boy loves how rowdy you make me feel."

As Zaire's comments sunk in, China grinned. "I'm not always naughty. You bring out the mischief in me."

"That's really good to know." Zaire kissed the tip of China's nose. "Your mischievousness is a real turn-on. Don't get mad if I push the naughty button too often."

"As far as *too often* is concerned, I'm not sure such a button exists."

He kissed her gently. Tenderly gripping her hips, holding on to her tightly, Zaire let China lead. Every time she lifted her buttocks, he thrust upward, burying his organ deeper. Enjoying the fiery responses, he was filled and beyond thrilled, thinking of more ways to pleasure her. Just so she'd know how hot she had him, he didn't try to control his jerking body, moaning loudly each time she rocked his world.

As China's body went into wild spasms, he felt as though her orgasm was coming straight through him. Excited by her purring moans and soft cooing, his own powerful release ripped recklessly through his body. They collapsed together.

"China, I love you." His whispered confession of love hadn't merely come from the riotous climaxes of their bodies. "I love you," he repeated. "I fell in love with you in an instant."

China was surprised by his confession of love, but she wasn't the least bit intimidated. "I love you, too, Zaire," she said, looking into his eyes, "from the bottom of my heart."

Emotionally moved by China's sincere declaration, Zaire's forefinger circled the area around her heart. "This is precious to me. I'll never intentionally break it."

"I believe you. I won't cause your heart any pain, either." Looking deeply into his eyes, her fingernail tenderly grazed across his lower lip. "I'm lucky to have you in my life."

Zaire nodded. "I feel the same."

Deciding it was time for a repeat performance, he hurried and put on another condom. Taking control of the situation, he turned China over onto her back. Looking down upon her breasts caused a quivering to erupt inside his belly. Twin mounds of firm brown flesh and hardened nipples drew his hand in like a magnet.

Gently palming each breast, he squeezed tenderly. "I can't believe I'm lying here with you like this. I love being with you. I love everything about you."

Using his fingertip, Zaire circled each of China's nipples. Lowering his head, he drew one into his mouth, sucking on it tenderly. "You taste so sweet." He loved how her breasts filled his hands and mouth. Zaire suckled her nipple again, his forefinger slowly traveling downward to her navel.

As Zaire entered China, he moaned from the pleasure. She tilted her hips, meeting eagerly each of his powerful thrusts. Losing her mouth to his, she basked in the passion his tongue brought to her. Every thrust and grind they made was deeper than the previous one, causing one hell of a firestorm.

Their earth-shattering climaxes came rapidly this time, each screaming out the other's name. Growing still, Zaire

stayed inside of China until his manhood completely softened. Upon withdrawal, a guttural moan escaped his throat.

After massaging Zaire's chest, China stimulated his nipples, causing them to pucker. Realizing she had no strength
for an encore, she stopped and lay perfectly still.

His heart overflowed with love and joy. "You are an
amazing woman. I'll hold you close to my heart forever.
I'll prove that I'm worthy of you."

Peering up at Zaire, China smiled. "I wanted you…and I
wasn't leaving this ranch without making love to you. Don't
try to complicate it, Zaire. Let's keep what we have as un-
complicated as possible. Complications are the last things
I want in my life."

"We can be all that you want us to be, China." He laid
his head between her breasts. "We still have lots of time
before you go home."

Moving his head higher and higher, Zaire captured with
his mouth the sweet taste of China's full lips. As his hands
roved over her soft skin, he felt her body tremble with
desire.

China and Zaire had only spent one full night together.
It had occurred outdoors in the elements, after the bonfire.
She hoped tonight would be another all-nighter for them,
but this time she wanted it to happen indoors either in her
cabin or his home. Despite the fact that he'd said he loved
her, Zaire had yet to invite her to his residence.

The couple made love again, growing more and more
tired with each stroke. The lovemaking was sweet and powerful, even if their bodies had lost steam.

A short time later, shaking like a leaf caught up in a
strong breeze, Zaire's third release came with an indescribable fury of spine-tingling sensations. Satiated from head
to toe, he breathlessly called out her name.

Feeling Zaire letting go, China patiently waited for her

body to finish spinning from a frenzy of delicious spasms. With his name on the tip of her tongue, she let it go.

Rolling over, she settled into his arms and gazed up at him. "It's late."

"I know." Zaire bowed his head, as if he were praying. "Come home with me?"

"I thought you'd never ask."

Chapter 9

Lots of glass and wood had been used in the decor throughout Zaire's spacious four-bedroom, three-bathroom home. Southwestern furnishings were featured in practically every room of the single-story structure, with the exception of the formal dining room and the state-of-the-art gym. China noticed how the rambling country-style kitchen was fully equipped with up-to-date stainless steel appliances.

Leading China to the back of the home where the master suite was, Zaire held on to her hand tightly. That she had agreed to spend the night still had him ecstatic.

Taking China's jacket from her hand, Zaire hung it on the back of a valet chair. After stripping off his coat, he put it on top of hers then rolled up his shirtsleeves.

Pulling China to him, Zaire kissed her gently on the mouth. "Get undressed while I run you a warm bath. I'll be right in there." He pointed at the double doors on the left side of the room. "A couple of robes are hanging in the walk-in closet. Feel free to use whichever one you want."

Smiling, China nodded, watching after him as he disappeared into the bathroom.

Taking off her blouse, she folded it and laid it on a leather storage bench situated in front of his king, four-poster bed. Dropping down to the plush-carpeted floor, she removed her shoes and pulled off her jeans. Leaving on her bra and panties, she neatly folded the rest of her clothes and put them with her shirt.

Instead of retrieving a robe from inside Zaire's closet, China removed one of his shirts from a hanger. She peeled away her silk undergarments before putting on the red Western-style shirt. Walking into the bathroom, she struck a sexy modeling pose, leaning against the door and laughing.

Zaire summoned China with a suggestive look. Watching her walk toward him was poetry in motion. He loved her wearing his shirt. There was so much sweet intimacy between them. He whistled. "My shirt looks better on you than me."

Zaire held out his hand and China took hold of it. Lowering the shirt down over her shoulders, he rained butter-soft kisses onto her bare flesh. In one fluid motion, he removed the garment. Lifting her, he settled her naked body down into the steamy water.

Seated on the side of the tub, Zaire picked up a nylon sponge and drenched it with liquid soap. Gently moving his hand around on her body in tantalizing circles, he covered every inch of her in the oversize tub. "Relaxed yet?"

"As soon as my body hit the water, I felt the tension split." She peered up at him. "Aren't you getting in?"

Throwing back his head, Zaire laughed. "Thought you'd never ask."

Tucking the sponge between her legs, he stood and hurriedly stripped out of his clothes. China was utterly mesmerized by his every movement. Settling down in the tub behind her, he guided her shoulders until her back rested against his chest.

Reaching for the sponge, Zaire began tenderly washing her. Since she wasn't panicking over her hair, he didn't worry about getting it wet.

Turning around to face Zaire, China straddled his thighs. Taking the sponge from his hand, she washed his arms and chest, slowly moving down to his sex. Loving the look of surrender on his handsome face, she smiled. "Feel good?"

"Damn…good," he said, struggling to swallow the lump in his throat. "I thought you might be a feisty one from the start, but you're something else."

A devilish gleam in her eyes, she watched him closely. "What might that something else be, Mr. Kingdom?"

Drawing her head forward, he tipped it until he could take her lower lip between his teeth, sucking on it. "Too much to name," he said in a sigh.

Moving her buttocks farther up on his thighs, China leaned in and laid her head on his soapy shoulder. "This is so unbelievable. I came to Texas to spread Daddy's ashes and to experience life on a ranch. This was supposed to be a vacation from my grief and fatigue. I didn't come here to fall in love. Yet I have, deeply, madly."

Lodging his fingers into her hair, he lifted China's face, kissing her hungrily. "We both fell in love. You're not in this alone, China. We don't know what tomorrow will bring, but we agreed to enjoy each other in real time. No one is even promised a tomorrow. Let's not develop hangups."

"Why do you always make perfect sense? No more hangups." Capturing Zaire's mouth with her own, China kissed him softly at first. Then she lost total control of her mouth, her kisses turning wet, hot and beyond passionate.

Awakening in Zaire's bed felt so natural to China. His side of the mattress was empty, but she felt sure he was somewhere in the house. Grabbing hold of his pillow, she hugged it to her, inhaling deeply. A whiff of his natural scent was mixed with his cologne. Thinking of their incredible night of lovemaking made her smile. While they'd made love three times in the hayloft, they'd only indulged once more. After a quick bath, they'd cuddled and held each other tight throughout the night.

Looking over at the bathroom door, China smiled brightly, recalling the unforgettable foreplay they'd shared in the tub. Zaire was the only man who'd bathed her.

Never before had she smelled the fragrant crystals and exotic oils he had poured into the steaming water. While washing every spot on her body, he'd also caressed her intimate zones with tender loving care.

"Good morning, beautiful." Zaire entered the room. Removing the pillow from her abdomen, he placed a breakfast tray across her lap. "How'd you sleep?"

"Morning, Zaire. I slept like a log." Beaming from head to toe, China gazed up at the man who'd been rocking her entire world. The heavenly smell of breakfast food wafted past her nose, causing her stomach to growl. "What did you expect to happen after you'd worn me out, depleting all my energy?"

Zaire grinned. "You sure know how to feed a man's ego. You wore me out, too."

China looked down at the food. "Pancakes and sausage. What a treat for me. I see you've been paying close attention to my babblings. The eggs are cooked just the way I like them. Are these biscuits from scratch?"

Zaire wished he'd made the bread. "I scratched them straight from the freezer. Mom keeps me in homemade biscuits. I only popped them into the oven. Eat up." He glanced over at the bedside clock. "I've got to get my food. Be right back."

Zaire was only gone for a few minutes. Returning to the room, he carried another breakfast tray. After getting comfortable in bed, he positioned the tray over his lap. "I have to leave in an hour or so, but you don't have to go. Stay as long as you'd like. I hope you'll be here when I get back."

China thought about his remarks. "You'll be gone all day. I can't stay that long. I have things to do."

Removing a key from a nightstand drawer, Zaire tossed it onto the bed. "Lock up when you leave. You can put the key under the doormat."

China was speechless. It thrilled her to know he trusted her that way, but it also made her uncomfortable. She couldn't imagine hanging out in his home when he wasn't there. It just didn't seem right.

Besides, she was leaving soon, and it may pose a problem for them. She'd eventually have to give back the key. No way could she stay after he left. "It's a generous offer, but I'm leaving when you do." Feeling extremely nervous, she began eating fast.

"Why not?" He hunched his shoulders.

"Zaire... I don't think you understand what I mean. We both know I'm leaving soon and I think it'll make things awkward for us. There's no reason I can't be ready to go when you are."

Zaire *did* understand. No one had to remind him China was leaving. It only occupied his thoughts day and night. What he'd do with himself after she left was still an unanswered question. He'd vowed not to bring up her leaving, but here it was staring him in the face again.

Zaire's work was his life, but somehow China had changed his course. He desired more than his work. He desperately wanted China in his life. "We'll leave together."

China's laughter was filled with relief. She hadn't hurt Zaire's feelings and she was happy about it. "I love being with you."

"Same goes for me. We can be together as often as possible, China."

Smiling, she blew him a kiss. "Thanks for making me welcome. I'm looking forward to us getting to know each other better."

"I like what I already know. But there's a lot more for us to learn about each other."

Happy that they'd managed to come to an agreeable end, China laid her head back onto the pillow. She felt tension drain from her body. "What's first on this Thursday morning's schedule? Tomorrow is Friday, the one week anniversary of my arrival."

"Only a week? Time flies." He kissed her. "Riding lessons are usually first. Since there aren't any classes on Sunday, we pack everything into six days. Our family tries hard to get together for church. We can't always make it happen, but we attend services as often as possible."

China looked embarrassed. "I don't get to church often enough. Sometimes I feel guilty about it, even if I watch a service on television. Daddy was a faithful servant, and he wanted me to be one."

Jabbing at his heart, Zaire gave her a look of understanding. "Church is inside the heart."

With tears floating in her pretty eyes, China smiled. "Thanks. I needed to hear that. You always find a way to shine a bright light."

He saw past her tears. "I love your smile, China. I never want to make you cry."

* * *

Wearing white Bermuda shorts and a yellow camp shirt, China slipped into a building where she checked out the wall guide for which room the quilting class was held in. Zaire's aunts Ethel and Josephine were the instructors.

A couple of minutes before class, China walked into the classroom and took a seat in the front row. Around ten female students were present, but none of Zaire's aunts had shown up yet. Seats suddenly began to fill up. China didn't know the first thing about quilting, but she recalled the stories Brody had told her about his mother's quilting talent. Marjorie Braxton was referred to as the "master quilter" in her tiny farm community.

Looking like a lovely spring day, the sisters walked in. *These ladies love soft colors,* China thought. Josephine and Ethel stood in front of the class. "Hello. It's nice to see you all this afternoon. I'm Josephine." She pointed at her sister. "This is Ethel. We're here to teach you fundamentals of quilting. It is loads of fun. You can use it as a hobby or as a moneymaker. My sisters and I use it for both. Our quilts are sold in the ranch's gift shop and at local bazaars."

Ethel held up a couple of items. "These tools are the most important ones used in quilting. This one is a rotary cutter. It is razor sharp and resembles a pizza cutter. This is a rotary mat, and it's used for cutting materials. We'll also introduce you to a tool known as a rotary ruler."

Paying close attention, China watched the women demonstrate the use of each tool. It didn't take her long to see how highly trained they were. Both women had extremely adept hands.

"Class, please follow us to the table in back. Bring your chairs with you," Ethel requested. "We'll first instruct you in the proper use of a design wall."

Appearing eager to get the class started, students moved quickly to the back table, dragging lightweight chairs behind them.

By the time China walked out of the classroom, her head was full of visions of colorful squares of material arranged in an array of patterns. The second China stepped outdoors, the heavens opened up. Buckets of rain poured down, accompanied by rolling thunder and flashes of lightning. She went back inside where other students waited for the rain to subside.

Suddenly China decided to just make a run for the cabin. Rushing headlong into the downpour, she laughed like a little girl. As hot as the outdoor temperature was, she couldn't believe the coolness of the torrential rains.

Running as fast as her legs would carry her, she reached the cabin within fifteen minutes of stepping out of the building. Soaked through and through, her clothing clung to her body like a second skin. She quickly came up with her key and ran into her cabin.

Wondering how many raindrops had already fallen from the skies, China stared out at the rain. She couldn't count the times she and Brody had taken walks in a downpour. But the rushing waterfall outside was far more than anything she'd been exposed to.

Heading for the bathroom, China stripped away her wet attire. She went in and turned on the shower, stepping into its downpour a few minutes later. Steaming water felt much better against her skin than the pelting rain had, but she had tremendously enjoyed the wet trek home.

Thinking of Zaire running alongside her in the rain gave China a warm rush. He was coming there after showering and changing clothes at the end of his workday. Since most of his classes were taught outdoors, she wondered if they'd been cancelled.

Not knowing when Zaire was coming, China vacated the bathroom. Looking at the bed, she thought about a nap. They had been quite active last evening and her body still hadn't fully recovered, despite a good night's sleep in Zaire's arms.

China just couldn't ignore the signals her body gave off, so she pulled back the bedding and lay down. Covering her nude frame with only the top sheet, she stared up at the ceiling, calling on her vivid memories of times spent in Zaire's company.

Standing at the cabin door, Zaire had already knocked three times. He went over to the porch swing and sat down. Pulling out his cell phone, he called the switchboard and asked to be connected to China's cabin.

Zaire knew exactly what he wanted and had no problem seeking it with a vengeance. He desperately wanted China Braxton, but he didn't have a clue how to pursue a city girl who had no desire for country living. She enjoyed all the amenities the ranch had to offer, but that's what people did on vacation. Having a good time was the reason patrons came to Whispering Lakes.

Remembering the pact he'd made last night about this very subject, Zaire willed his mind from the troubling issue. *Thoroughly enjoy China now. Deal with the aftermath of her departure once she is no longer available for me to reach out and touch.*

Zaire frowned. "I woke you. I'm sorry. Call me when you get up."

"I can talk now. With all the rain, I didn't know when you'd get here so I lay down. Where are you?"

Chuckling, Zaire stood, walked over to the door and rang

the bell. "Right outside your cabin, sweetheart. Please let me in."

China giggled. "Pronto!"

Slipping out of bed, she reached for a silk robe. While slipping on the garment, she dashed to the front door. Zaire was outside, and she could hardly wait to fall into his arms. The possibility of him wondering why she was wearing only a robe crossed her mind fleetingly. She then reminded herself that he already knew she'd been asleep.

Chewing on a sliver of straw, Zaire leaned against the porch's wooden post, his eyes hungrily devouring the sexy woman clad in white silk. The couple came together, hugging, kissing and holding each other close. Taking Zaire by the hand, she led him inside the cabin.

Zaire suddenly came to a halt. "I've got to get something out of the SUV."

Curious about what he had to retrieve, China sat down on the sofa to wait for him. Thinking she should put on underwear, worried that he might think she was too provocative, she got up. Zaire walked back in before she could do anything about her state of undress. At least her robe covered everything. Thinking of his hands slipping under the robe to caress her bare flesh infused her cheeks with color.

He noticed the sudden rosiness in her cheeks. "What's that look all about?"

China laughed softly. "You don't want to know. Are those pizzas?" she asked, quickly changing the subject.

"Pizza it is. Get the paper plates."

"I can bring them in here if you want."

"We can eat in the kitchen. What do you have cold?"

"Strawberry lemonade and Coca-Cola."

"I'll take the lemonade."

Zaire followed China into the kitchen, setting the boxes on the table. He then pulled out two chairs.

Opening the refrigerator, China carefully removed a glass pitcher of lemonade and a Coke for herself. She set the items on the table before dropping down onto a chair.

The delicious aroma of fresh tomato sauce drifted from the boxes. "This is a vegetarian pizza with sun-dried tomatoes, black olives and mushrooms. The other one is loaded with pepperoni and mushrooms. Both have extra cheese."

"I'll have a slice of each," China said.

"There's plenty, so don't be shy."

China snickered. "I'm not ashamed to fill up."

Zaire laughed. "That's my girl!"

After finding out what kind of pizza Zaire preferred, China removed one slice of each and placed them on a paper plate. Taking a couple of napkins from a wooden holder, she handed everything over to Zaire.

"Thanks, China. I like being waited on by you."

"Aren't you used to it? I'm sure your mom caters to her guys."

"That's different. I haven't dined with someone special, other than you, in a long time."

"Why is that?"

"Other than the ladies in my family, I haven't eaten a meal with a member of the opposite sex in a long time. I changed when you came along. Opening up and acting on my attraction to you came easy for me but it was scary."

China raised an eyebrow. "Why scary?"

"Change always comes with its share of phobias, China. My family is both shocked and thrilled to see me shed my cocoon."

China smiled. "I'm glad you broke out."

He nodded. "You helped with that…and in a big way. I feel liberated."

China couldn't help wondering if he'd go back into his shell after she left. Because they'd agreed not to discuss her departure, she didn't ask the questions burning in her mind. "Have you ever been in love?"

Fleeting shards of pain flickered in and then out of Zaire's eyes. "There was someone special once. We didn't work out for the same old reasons. It's always been my desire to live on the ranch, and I've never failed to voice my intent. Although I held a full-time job in Brownsville, no one I ever dated warmed to the idea of ending up way out here. One woman referred to this place as a desert of desolation."

"That's kind of dark. There's as much life out here as anywhere. People are all over the place. The ranch gets more than its fair share of guests and the activities are fun. Any future plans to expand?" Picking up a slice of pizza, she bit off a chunk.

Zaire swallowed his food. "I want to build a state-of-the-art movie theater. We have a space where guests get together to watch DVDs. But I want movie-style seating, a silver screen with surround sound. A video arcade, a bowling alley and another swimming pool are included in future plans."

"Why another pool when there are so many great lakes to take a dip in?"

Zaire chuckled. "Some of our lakes are too dangerous for swimming. The steep drop-offs make them unsafe. One moment your feet are on solid ground. Then, all of a sudden, there's no ground to stand on."

"Hmm, I see how that can be dangerous. Any other grandiose plans?"

"Grandiose, huh? I don't see it like that. I focus on one project at a time, especially the *grandiose* ones," he said, laughing. "The movie theater is the meal on my plate right now. My brothers agree with the addition. We're in the process of getting building costs, time estimates and other important project information."

"Won't adding new additions take away the theme or mystique of rustic living on a dude ranch?"

Zaire was impressed with her line of questioning. "We've thought of it…and it has been discussed. We'd never compromise the ranch's main objectives, but it's important to keep up with change to remain competitive. A movie theater can only enhance our current offerings."

"Seems you've put a lot of thought into it, Mr. Kingdom. I wish you well. Now, when do you plan to take me to South Padre Island?"

Zaire chortled. "Your memory is sharp as a tack. We can go tomorrow if one of my brothers or Morgan can cover for me. We can celebrate your first week. Are we on?"

Nodding eagerly, China grinned. "We're on!"

A full pizza and a half was consumed by China and Zaire. Removing the remaining slices from the boxes, she stored them in a plastic container to put in the refrigerator. Zaire had nearly drained the pitcher of lemonade.

As the couple walked into the living room to relax, Zaire slipped an arm around China's slender waist. The thin material exposed her sizzling nakedness to his touch. Walking over to the three-way lamp, he dimmed it, instantly creating a romantic ambiance. He then put on a CD of CW love ballads.

They took seats on the sofa. China leaned over and laid her head upon Zaire's broad shoulder. "This feels nice. I like quiet. The romantic atmosphere is alluring. I burn lots of candles even when I'm alone."

"Speaking of alone, I recall asking if you had a man in your life. You said you didn't have a lifetime partner and I backed off. What about a *here for now* partner? Do you have one of those?"

Cupping his face between both her hands, China kissed Zaire softly on the mouth. "Yes, I do. It's you, Mr. Kingdom. You're the only one who stimulates my appetite."

"That's nice to know." Zaire gave China a lingering kiss, quietly thinking about her response. Taking this conversation any further could easily turn a tenderly soft mood into an ugly, uncomfortable one. Unwilling to risk ruining the moment, he abandoned the probing expedition.

Removing his boots, Zaire shifted his position on the sofa, disturbing China momentarily. Leaving on his socks, he stretched out, pressing his back into the sofa back. Directing her to lie down with him, he gently pulled her into him, tossing his arm across her abdomen. "This *is* nice, real nice," Zaire whispered.

China turned and twisted until their bodies were perfectly aligned. Staring into his eyes, she felt hypnotized by the love and warmth he gazed back at her with. "You are a special man." *You're a special man who needs a very special lady at your side. I want to be that special somebody to you, but I don't know how to accomplish it.*

"You're pretty special yourself." He lifted several strands of her hair and twirled it around his finger. "Meeting you has been a blessing."

"I feel the same as you do, Zaire. I don't know exactly what's in store for us, but I think about it a lot. We like each other so much. I hope we'll know each other long after my vacation ends." This moment was so tender that China's eyes filled with tears.

Zaire kissed away her tears. "I want that, too, China. It can happen for us. We'll eventually come to know what's in store for us. You can be sure of it. Mom taught us to wait instead of acting out rashly and impatiently."

Closing his eyes, Zaire's fingers stroked the length of her hair. As he recalled the triple lovemaking sessions of the previous evening, his sex hardened. He was sure China had felt its expansion. Not wanting her to think he was there just for sex, he didn't do anything at all to act upon his deep desire. Talking to her and sharing quiet moments together was enough.

China wondered what Zaire was thinking. Tilting her head back, she saw that his eyes were still shut. The stroking of her hair had slowed considerably. He was well on his way to slumberland. Despite the earlier rainfall, he had put in a hard day's work. Managing a place this size had to be backbreaking. China knew that running Whispering Lakes Ranch was a labor of love for Zaire.

Pressing her fingers to her lips, China kissed them and blew the sweet affection toward Zaire's mouth. She'd love for them to lie down in bed together, but he looked far too comfortable for her to disturb. If she awakened him, he might have a hard time getting back to sleep.

Content to have Zaire lying there with her and feeling totally at peace, China closed her eyes. Should they awaken in the wee hours of the morning, she hoped he'd want to move into her bed instead of out the door. Since they'd stayed together last night, China believed there was a good chance they'd awaken in each other's arms.

Awakening to soft kisses and whispers of warm breath near her ear, China reached up and put her arms around Zaire's neck. Pulling his head down until their lips met, she'd never been happier. A glance at the clock radio told her it was a few minutes after three in the morning. While peering into his eyes, she thought about what Zaire meant to her. How could she want another person so badly, yet not make whatever compromises it took to get him? Pushing all thoughts to the side, she opened her mouth to receive his probing tongue.

Zaire's kiss was sweeter than pure honey.

Chapter 10

Dressed in a dainty orange sundress with an orange-and-white bikini beneath it, China was seated on the porch swing. The colorful straw tote she'd loaded with sunscreen, baby oil, a novel and magazines was on the top step. She had also packed a just-in-case change of clothing.

Zaire had called twenty minutes ago to say he was on his way back to pick her up for the trip to South Padre Island. China expected him any minute. He had left her cabin only a couple of hours ago, shortly after they'd made love and showered.

Instead of waiting inside the cabin, China had come outside. It was too nice a day to be cooped up inside. A bright sun was high and the Texas sky was blue and clear.

Hearing the familiar sounds of a vehicle, China leapt to her feet. Though she was pretty sure it was Zaire, a quick glance down the road confirmed it. Instead of his truck, he was driving the SUV.

China stepped off the porch and walked to the paved road. Eager to be in Zaire's intoxicating company, her heartbeat raced. Unable to keep her smile undercover, she let it shine brightly. This was yet another new day for them.

Memories of their past evenings kept her company as she continued walking.

Thinking of Zaire awakening in the wee hours of the morning made her smile broadly. He'd lifted her from the sofa and carried her to bed. She'd been awake during the transfer but she'd remained quiet and perfectly still, basking in the strength of his tender arms.

Watching him hastily undressing by the moonlight shining through the bedroom window had been an amazing experience. As soon as he'd stripped out of his attire, he had joined her in bed. Shortly after bringing her into his strong arms, they'd made sweet love. The pace was slow and tantalizing, filled with tenderness, warmth and compassion.

The second time around was wild and crazy, as they fully explored each other's bodies. Both China and Zaire had eventually fallen asleep from extreme fatigue, but not before he'd caressed her with such tenderness. She had utterly basked in the afterglow of his tender lovemaking.

China hoped today would be as scintillating as the previous days and nights. The heightened passion she felt at just seeing Zaire already topped the charts. She wasn't interested in playing games. All she wanted to do was make every second of their time together memorable.

Leaving the engine running, Zaire got out of the SUV and ran over to China.

Lifting her in his arms, he swung her around. "You're a bright ray of sunshine. Ready to hit the road?"

"Ready as I'll ever be." She eyed him up and down, appreciating his fine physique. "What's under those dark shorts? Are you wearing swim trunks?"

Zaire laughed heartily. "As a matter of fact, I am. Why do you ask?"

China shrugged. "Just wondering if you'd have to change clothes once we got to the beach. Watching you strip down again would be nothing short of marvelous."

Zaire grinned in response to her answer. "Let's go. Don't want this day to get away from us."

Once China was seated in the SUV, Zaire secured her door then ran to the driver's side. After buckling his seat belt he turned the radio down to be heard. "Any particular station or CD you want to hear?"

China smiled lazily. "Anything soft and inspiring will do, but nothing that'll put me to sleep. I want to be awake to see everything."

He loved her enthusiasm. "I'm with you on that, kiddo. And I definitely can't fall asleep with precious cargo aboard. You *are* precious to me, you know."

China glowed. "I know." Zaire's words made her happy, yet her heart suddenly felt sad. The bliss would be over way too soon. *One week left.* "You're precious to me, too."

China's response zipped jaggedly through Zaire. He hadn't heard any conviction in her tone. The statement had fallen totally flat. Getting her to truly fall in love with him and Texas wasn't looking too promising.

Today, Zaire thought, get through today. Then see what tomorrow brings. Until China expressed a desire for a long-term relationship, he couldn't push the envelope.

Zaire pulled into the valet lane of the Villa Grande Hotel and parked.

China gave him a puzzled look. "Why are we parking here? We're going to the beach, right?"

"No doubt. I reserved a room so we can shower and change later. I thought we'd have dinner at a nice restaurant. We'll check out of the hotel after we eat."

China's expression softened at his thoughtfulness. "You think of everything." China liked how he took control.

"Glad you approve," he said sarcastically.

China picked up on his change in mood. She'd hurt his feelings. "Sorry I questioned you like that. I was rude."

Without responding, Zaire got out of the vehicle. After unloading a leather hang-up bag, he moved aside for an attendant to take over.

Zaire walked around the SUV and took hold of China's satchel. "You can sit in the lobby while I check in." Without saying a word, he strolled off.

Slightly insulted by his immaturity, China walked behind him. The day she'd been looking forward to was becoming a drag. Neither of them would have a good time if bad moods presided. Zaire was definitely in a funk—and she was the cause of it.

The lobby was colorful, as were the cushions on the beautiful wicker sofas and chairs. China took a seat where she could look out the window. Much to her surprise, the coast was visible. She'd had no idea this hotel had its own private beach.

Summoning China with his hand, Zaire kept his eyes glued to her as she walked toward him. As his pulse quickened, he knew he couldn't help these strong reactions to her. She was the most interesting and sexiest woman he'd ever met.

Hoping to lighten his mood, China took hold of his arm. "This is a beautiful place. I guess you already know what I saw when I peered out the window."

Zaire nodded. "You'll love it here. This stretch of beach is exclusive to hotel guests. I wanted this day to be wonderful for you."

"It will be...for both of us. Thanks for wanting me to be happy. This is the happiest I've been in a long time." Want-

ing Zaire to know just how he'd made her feel, she stood
on tiptoes and kissed him gently on the mouth. "Thanks
for making this happen. All of it, since day one."

Zaire felt instant relief. He'd been fearful that the outing
had hit rock bottom. Seeing her smile was like a ray of sunshine on a dreary day. Hope welled within him.

The hotel suite Zaire had booked was beautiful, with its
balcony overlooking the Gulf of Mexico. China imagined
the room was expensive, even more so since they weren't
spending the night. Booking a room for just several hours
was a lavish gesture.

Wearing dark blue swimming trunks and a dark T-shirt,
Zaire came out of the bathroom, interrupting China's
thoughts. "I'm ready to hit the water."

For several seconds China was speechless. She'd seen
him in the nude, yet his sculpted body and powerful thighs
in trunks made her tremble. For a distraction, China emp-
tied her satchel of everything unnecessary. The chances of
reading were slim. This day was sunny and beautiful, perfect for frolicking in the water and laying out on the sand.

"I'm ready," she announced, her voice sounding weak
and small.

Zaire had chosen a perfect location for them to hang
out. After paying the rental fees for two beach loungers,
a striped umbrella and a small table, he trudged back to
where he'd left China to claim their spot.

As soon as everything was situated, the couple ran into
the surf, laughing and splashing one another. It was like
the day had started all over for them. China was in heaven.

Seeing the enchanted look upon China's face, Zaire
reached for her, bringing her into his arms. His need for
her was stronger than anything he'd ever felt.

Wrapping her arms around Zaire's neck, China meshed her mouth against his, kissing him with fervor. Locking her fingers behind his head, she fought the fire of desire burning within her. If it was legal to make love on the beach, she'd gladly surrender her body to him. Loving Zaire and breathing seemed synonymous. If she chose breathing over loving, she wasn't sure that that alone would keep her alive.

Losing thoughts of everything but each other as if they were the only two people on the beach, Zaire and China continued holding one another, caressing and kissing. She filled him up and he did the same for her, yet she still wanted more and more of him. Her heart overflowing with love for a man was a new experience.

Carrying China out of the water, Zaire laid her down on one of the loungers. After drying her off he took sunscreen from her satchel and sprayed a good amount into his hands. Oiling her down from head to toe put him in a bad way physically. Making love to her would be the only solution to tamping down his manhood.

"Aren't you putting on any sunscreen?" China asked him.

"Don't need it. This dark chocolate won't burn, babe."

"It might melt. And I'd love to be the one to lick it off your sexy body." Blushing, she laughed at herself.

Zaire thought China's idea was amazing. She could have her way with him.

"What…the hell…" Zaire yelped, feeling something cool on his back.

Laughing hard, China set down the container. Her straddling him on the lounger kept him from jumping up. "Relax, Zaire. It's only sunscreen. It can't hurt you."

China's hands tenderly massaging Zaire's back knocked him into a state of bewildered silence. Her fingers felt magical, hot and dangerous against his bare flesh.

Using the pads of her thumbs, China tenderly kneaded the back of Zaire's neck. As she gently ran the tip of her fingernail up and down his spine, he gritted his teeth to keep from yelping out again. If making him feel good was her mission, she was accomplishing it in spades.

"How does that feel?" she whispered softly.

"Great! Your hands are soothing."

She frowned. "Is that all?"

"They're also strong and stimulating. The strength in your fingers is amazing. I'm starting to feel drowsy. Come lie down and join me for a nap."

China wore a scowl on her face, but he couldn't see it. "A nap, after all the tenderness you just received? You've got to be kidding!"

Zaire suppressed his laughter. "Please lie down with me. I want to feel the heat of your body all over mine."

The moment China got off him he turned over on his back. Then he pulled her down on top of him, silencing her pursed lips with a moist kiss. With their bodies squeezed together on one lounger, China and Zaire clung to each other.

Under the South Padre sun, they found joy with each other. This idyllic, romantic beach setting was perfect for them. After thirty minutes of lying quietly next to Zaire, China raised her head. Looking out over the water, her lips slowly curved into a dazzling smile. Rolling whitecaps were a fascinating sight. Crystal blue waters appeared to stretch into eternity. Blue skies above appeared never ending. This is one beautiful day, she thought.

Hearing happy laughter trilling from nearby adults and children was heartwarming to China. Light jazz drifted on the air via Zaire's portable CD player. Using her hands to shade her eyes, she looked farther down the beach. Much to her surprise, she saw several horses galloping along in shallow waters, guided by riders. Riding horseback up and down the coastline looked like fun.

Leaning her head over Zaire, she blew into his ear. "Wake up, sleepyhead. There's something exciting you've got to see."

Zaire opened one eye and then the other. Taking his good old time, he managed to pull himself up into a sitting position. Looking in the direction China was pointing, he saw exactly what she was gaga over. "Beautiful, isn't it? This is a normal sight for folks around these parts. Horseback riding on the beach is offered by the owners of nearby stables. I'd worry about cleaning up the waste, but the city seems to take care of everything. The beaches down here are always kept in pristine condition."

"I don't get to see this on L.A. beaches. It's pretty exciting. Do you think we could take a ride?"

Zaire grinned. "One or two horses?"

China chuckled. "One, of course. I'm still nowhere close to anything but a beginner rider."

"For you to have the total experience, I think we need to rent two horses. Like before, I'll be there to guide you… and the stable guides are always present. They don't leave these precious animals in the hands of tourists. They also know which beach areas are off-limits to riders."

China looked around at their belongings. "What should we do with our stuff?"

"It'll be okay. But if you'll feel better, I'll ask the family closest to us to watch over our things. We won't be gone long."

"What if they say no?"

Laughing, Zaire shook his head from side to side. "Let's cross that bridge if we come to it. Most Texans are kind, decent folks. If they say no, we'll just take everything up to the room."

"I haven't run into any mean-looking, black-hat-wearing Texans."

Zaire looked puzzled.

"You know how in the Westerns good cowboys wear white hats and bad ones wear black," China explained. "I love to watch old Westerns."

Fully understanding her comment, Zaire nodded in agreement. "That's the way it is. Everything seems to come down to black and white." Zaire got to his feet. "We'd better get started if we're renting horses. The rental area is at the other end of the beach." He pointed out the stables.

Zaire eyed her bikini. "Do you have any sort of pants in that straw bag of yours?"

"I packed a pair of capri pants. Will those do?"

"Anything to cover your upper legs will work."

Reaching into the satchel, she pulled out the orange capri pants and quickly slipped them on. Thinking of the very simple but sexy black dress she'd brought along had her heaving a sigh of relief. It was perfect for evening dining.

Zaire reported back to China that the neighboring family was happy to watch their belongings.

The entire scene was extremely hard for China to take in. She'd never seen anything like it. Stables and corrals erected on a beach. This was unheard of in her home state.

Once the attendants gave out important instructions to the riders, Zaire and China were appointed a guide and a small group to ride single file with. It'd make it easy for Zaire to lead China's horse, but he hoped she'd take control. If she did, he knew she'd never regret or forget it.

In confidence, Zaire had asked an attendant to assign China the gentlest filly, but with one stipulation. The horse had to be alive and breathing. The attendant had laughed at Zaire's great sense of humor.

"Zaire, please hand me the reins. I'd like to see if I can handle it on my own."

Zaire smiled broadly. "With pleasure. Believe in yourself and your mount will believe in you. Doubt yourself… and he'll take charge. We don't want that to happen."

Taking a firm hold of the reins, China smiled reassuringly. Bending forward, she whispered into the horse's ear. "Nightingale, do as I say and we'll get along just fine. I'm in charge. Keep that in mind."

Nodding her head up and down, the dark brown filly whinnied as if it understood China's remarks. The couple cracked up.

Fifteen minutes into the ride China had decided that this was truly an amazing experience. She felt good about herself, glad she'd so boldly taken over the reins. Zaire had already told her several times how proud he was of her. She believed him. Pride for her was in his eyes.

As the horses picked up speed, China panicked for a brief moment. Pulling herself up straight in the saddle, she snapped the reins with authority, bracing herself. When Nightingale took off she knew China was in control and performed accordingly. Giddy with pleasure and pride, she winked at Zaire, mouthing a silent thank you. Had it not been for him and his patient teachings, she wouldn't even be on a horse.

There were many things she was grateful to him for. In her wildest dreams she'd never thought of herself as a cowgirl living out her life on a huge Texas spread.

Fighting sleep, China did her best to stay awake, using a small amount of eyeliner and waterproof mascara to perk up her eyes. Her tan was deep enough that she didn't have to use any foundation. Golden-peach blush to her cheeks and a bronze gloss to her lips was all she needed to make her features shimmer with color.

China didn't know what she would've done with her hair without the hotel-owned blow-dryer. Once she'd washed it and blown it dry, she'd used her flatiron on it.

Zaire had thoroughly dried off after a hot shower and had put on his briefs. Seated on the side of a king-size bed, he pulled on a pair of dark socks. Instead of his cowboy boots, he'd brought along a regular pair of dark brown dress shoes to complement the dressy dinner attire he planned to wear.

Getting to his feet, Zaire walked over to the mirror, peering into it as he slipped on a pair of brown slacks and buttoned his beige-and-brown-striped dress shirt.

Evenings on South Padre Island could turn rather cool, so he'd brought along a blazer. He hoped China had packed a sweater or jacket of some sort. If not, he had no problem giving her his.

Coming out of the bathroom, China took one look at Zaire and instantly stopped.

She hadn't seen him in anything but a variety of Western gear, except for the night he'd come to dinner, and even then his attire had been casual-dressy.

Walking over to Zaire, China ran her fingertips up and down his arm. "You look great, Zaire! I really like you in dress clothes." She saw him lift his eyebrows. "Don't get me wrong now. I love seeing you in jeans and Western shirts, but it's my first time seeing you this dressed up."

"Like city folks, huh?"

China rolled her eyes. "If that's how you want to take it, but that's not what I meant."

"Oh, you were more than clear." Leaning in to her, he gave her a sweet kiss on the forehead. "I like how you look, too. That little dress is sexy. Men will be looking at your amazing figure. I can't imagine how anyone could let your natural beauty go unnoticed." He kissed her again. "How's your appetite?"

"For what?" She smiled wryly.

"Food! What else?"

Feeling rather bold and sexy, she purred softly. "I'm hungry, but I'm hungrier for the feel and taste of you." She put one of her fingernails to her temple. "Since you have to pay for this room in full, maybe we could check out early in the morning. I think we'll be better after a good night's sleep."

Laughing, Zaire threw up his hands. "Honest to goodness, staying overnight wasn't my intent. I booked the room for the reasons I told you." He cupped her face in his hands. "But to tell the truth, I'm glad you want to stay. Checkout is around noon. Is that too late for us to leave?"

She smiled. "I have nowhere to go. We'll leave whenever you say."

His smile was broad. "Good. Let's get out of this room. I'm seriously tempted to have my dessert before dinner."

"Good idea. My mind was on the same thing," China playfully cooed. Wrapping her arms around his neck, she kissed him passionately, giving him an idea of what to look forward to later. She hadn't lied about being hungry for him. In fact, it seemed to her as if she had an insatiable appetite for Zaire Kingdom.

Holding hands, Zaire and China followed along behind the hostess escorting them to their table.

Once they were seated, China surveyed the stylish decor. The candlelit tables adorned with white linens set the restaurant apart from casual dining facilities. The pianist in the corner was a great addition to an already first-class establishment.

Zaire eyed China. "I see you're checking out the place. Do you approve?"

Nodding, she smiled sweetly. Reaching across the table, she briefly placed her hand over his. "I love it, Zaire. It's relaxing, romantic and the soft piano music is soul soothing. And we can see the Gulf of Mexico from our window. And I'm crazy over most seafood. I highly approve."

"I'm pleased." Zaire smiled warmly.

They both ordered prime rib, lobster and wine, then settled in for the wait.

While Zaire closely studied China's body language, a strange mood slowly assailed him. Then he quickly figured out that it was time for him to get real with her. Reaching across the table, he took hold of China's hand. "I constantly think about how perfect we are together."

"It crosses my mind, too."

Zaire's gaze was strong and steady. "I'm lonely as hell, China. I've felt this way a good bit of my life. My mother, brothers and aunts have always been attentive to me, but I didn't and don't have close friends. And I've been wary of the opposite sex since grade school. Trusting comes hard for me. There are women and then there are *women*."

As raw pain filled Zaire's dark eyes China's heart felt like it was being shredded. "Which category of women do I fit into, the first or last?"

"The one I emphasized. You're a very good woman— and probably a whole lot more than that. When you leave Whispering Lakes, I'm afraid I'll go back to losing myself to the dark loneliness, possibly never to be found again. Please listen so I can get this question out while my courage is up. Can I visit you in Los Angeles?"

Looking into his eyes, she allowed his question to register in her mind and heart. "I'd really like that, Zaire. Anytime you want to come to L.A. just let me know. I'd love to have you." China wondered who'd hurt him so badly, sure that someone had.

Zaire was utterly relieved. "I can do that, no problem. Before you leave, maybe I should make up a list of foods I love to eat, including favorite snacks," he joked, hoping to lighten up things.

"Good idea. Another issue settled," she said, "and not a moment too soon. The waiter's heading this way."

"Perfect timing." Zaire grinned over his good fortune. He wanted to go to Los Angeles to see China and she wanted him to come. He couldn't ask for more. There were other important things he had to tell her, but he'd wait to see how things gelled for them.

The waiter went about his job of setting out the first course, bread and salad.

Hungrier than either had thought, they nearly inhaled the salads and bread.

The first bite of prime rib pleased China's palate. "So tender." She dipped a piece of meat into creamy horseradish sauce. "This is really good. How is yours?"

"As good as yours." He chuckled. "It *is* tender. Someone in the kitchen knows how to rattle pots and pans. Mom and Morgan would enjoy the food here. Maybe I'll bring them down for their anniversary in late October."

"That'll be nice. Wish I could be here for the celebration."

His eyes filled with light. "I can arrange it. I'd love to fly you down for the anniversary party Zurich and Hailey are planning."

Though somewhat startled by the offer, China couldn't deny that she wanted to come back. Making too many future plans might be dangerous but she was willing to risk it. "When I get home, I'll check the vacation schedule. I'll need exact dates."

The pleased look on China's face put a smile on Zaire's lips. From her expression, he was sure he hadn't ruined the relaxed, fun-loving mood of the night.

China felt good being in Zaire's arms. They *were* a perfect fit. As the soft music pleasured their ears the couple moved with ease over the dance floor along with numerous other patrons. She hadn't seen any guests from the ranch, which was surprising since this was the day for the South Padre Island tour.

China was hoping to work off a heap of dinner calories. She had also declined dessert. Just as Zaire planned to use her to satisfy his sweet-tooth, China had every intention of ordering him for her after-dinner treat.

The music suddenly switched from soft and soothing to a more upbeat, funky and fast tempo. China looked over at the piano, but the pianist was gone. Locating the area where the music came from, she saw the piano player standing over a keyboard. Other musicians had joined him on a raised platform in the back of the room.

For someone who didn't socialize much, Zaire was light and smooth on his feet.

China recalled him saying his aunts learned the latest dance steps by watching television.

Maybe they taught him new dances. Visualizing him dancing with his lively aunts made her laugh.

He pulled her closer to him. "What's so funny?" he whispered near her ear.

"Just a few thoughts running through my head."

"Like what?"

"Imagining you and your aunts dancing together," she answered honestly. "Does that occur?"

Light danced in his eyes. "It does." Making sure China could hear him above the music, Zaire brought her closer to him. "It's hard to say no to them. Those sisters keep up with the latest dance moves. Music-video channels and *Dancing with the Stars* are their favorites. They watch too much television if you ask me."

"They've earned the right to do whatever they like," China said.

"And they do it all," he said with a chuckle.

Even though the song was fast-paced, Zaire kept China in his arms. Laying her head against his broad chest, she wrapped her arms around his waist.

China felt safe. Zaire possessed a quiet strength and he wasn't the kind of man who ran off at the mouth. China knew she was protected because Zaire Kingdom was a strong man of action.

After China let Zaire know she was ready to go, he steered her through the crowd and back to their table. Once he pulled out her chair, he looked around for the waiter and summoned him with a wave of his hand. Eager to get the check settled, he sat down across from China.

Zaire picked up his wineglass. "I'd like to offer a toast." He waited until she had her glass in hand. "Happy anniversary! You've survived your first week. I hope next week will be everything you want it to be."

Smiling, China tipped her glass toward his. "I'm sure it'll be all that and more."

China liked how attentive and polite Zaire was to her and others. Being scared was senseless she told herself, yet she knew how deep she was in with him. There were bound to be relationship issues for them to address. And they would come sooner rather than later because of the short vacation time she had left.

Zaire smiled gently. "The waiter is on his way back."

"I know."

"We'll be on our way in just a few minutes, China," Zaire assured her.

Chapter 11

Yawning, China stretched her hands high up over her head. She was sleepy but she wanted to stay awake to be with Zaire. While he was in the bathroom changing clothes, she slipped out of her dress and slid into bed. Since she hadn't brought along any sleepwear, she'd have to sleep in her bra and panties or in nothing at all. The latter was more appealing since Zaire would sleep next to her, but she kept on her underwear.

Reaching over to the lamp on the night table, she dimmed it. As Zaire came out of the bathroom she pulled the comforter up over her. Smiling at him, she summoned him with a crook of her finger. "I missed you."

"I missed you, too. I see you're settled in. How does the mattress feel?"

China bounced up and down. "It's in pretty good shape. No lumps."

Zaire smiled charmingly. "I'm ready to try it out."

Sprinting across the room, Zaire slipped into bed with China. Her warmth heated him up right away. Laying his head in her lap, he looked up at her. Pulling her head down until their lips met, Zaire kissed China thoroughly. Feeling like she was floating on air, she kissed him back.

Trying to get more comfortable, China slid farther down in bed, placing a plump pillow under her head. As she lay back Zaire pressed his face against her abdomen, sprinkling it with moist kisses. His desire for her couldn't be contained. Wanting China every time he looked at her or touched her had nothing to do with how long he'd been abstinent. His unyielding yearning was all about the woman she was and the wonderful way she made him feel.

Zaire reached out to her. "Come here, China. I want you."

China's eyes glowed with passion. "I'm glad 'cause I want you, too."

China lay on her stomach and rested her chin on his chest. While trailing a line of kisses down the middle of his chest she felt his labored breathing. Flicking at his nipples with her tongue caused him to squirm. Knowing she had aroused him made her want him even more.

Reaching inside his briefs, she massaged him tenderly, loving the hardening of his manhood against her palm. Touching him like this excited her. Turning Zaire on turned her on, too. Tugging at his briefs, she moved them down over his waist, hips and feet. "A condom," she whispered. "I hope you have a condom."

Zaire did have protection, but his wallet was in his pants in the bathroom. "I have to get up." He hated interrupting this tender moment but protecting them was a must.

China frowned. "For what?"

Grinning, he slipped out of bed. "A condom."

Laughing, China sat up and leaned back against the headboard to wait for him.

Taking things a step further, China took off her bra and panties then covered her body with the top sheet. She already knew he was ready to make love to her by the hardness of his sex. When he came back, he'd find out just how ready she was to take him over and over again.

China's attention was drawn to Zaire's figure as he made his way across the room. Slipping into bed, he reached for her. Feeling her nakedness, he was pleased by what he perceived as her wanting to get right down to it. Zaire moaned softly. "China, China, what are you doing to me? Having you in my life is all I think about."

Gently China ran her hand up and down his smooth shaft, kissing him at the same time. Feeling out of control felt good to her since she had always prided herself on being in control. Her mind dictated delicious things for her to carry out on him and her body happily obliged. Using her thumb, she smoothed it over the crown of his manhood. Bending her head, she kissed the flesh on both sides of his sex.

China admitted to herself that making love to Zaire was now an everyday occurrence. *This is just another day, another perfect day to make wild, passionate love to a dreamboat.*

Silencing her mind, China went back to the act of seducing the man lying next to her. Positioning herself on top of him, she bent her head and had her way with the sweetest lips she'd ever tasted. The tongue was a wonderful tool in the art of seduction. Every time her tongue touched his naked flesh, he shivered. He looked as if he was climbing his way toward heaven. His expression was erotic and arousing to her.

Rocking back on her knees, China positioned herself

to ease down onto his manhood and lock him within her. Trapping him inside her was a beautiful thing, one that made her barely able to wait. With moisture flowing from her intimate treasure, she slowly lowered herself until he was buried deep inside her.

A loud gasp escaped China as she united her femininity with his pleasure-evoking tool. As long and hard as it was, she wasn't sure her being on top was the best way to execute this lovemaking session. Rapidly she dismissed any misgivings. They wanted each other, and it was all that mattered in this overly heated moment in time. Going deeper and deeper and pulling back slightly, China teased him over and over again.

Zaire quickly flipped the script on her. Rolling her off him, he lay on top of her. He pinned her hands over her head with his. She eagerly let him have his way with her body, fully trusting the sexiest man on the planet.

Hovering slightly above China's body, Zaire gently lowered himself until he was right at the door of her womanhood. Feeling the moisture flowing from her, he slowly entered. As he tenderly plunged in and out of her passionate moans rushed from between his generous lips. Gripping her hips, he ground into her with tender force. China rose up to meet his deep thrusts.

Wrapping her legs around his waist, China trailed the tips of her nails up and down the small of his back, making him tremble. As his thrusts grew in intensity she lay back and let him ride her tender body like it was his first and last time. Over and over, she opened her mouth to receive his tongue, feeling her lips melting under the pressure of his hot kisses. "Take me, Zaire," she cried out. "You…feel so good…inside of me. Please…love me until…all…our strength…is gone."

The loud gasping between China's words let Zaire know

how much she enjoyed having him locked deep inside her. "I'll give…you whatever…you want, baby. Just tell me… what you need." His own gasps began. "You're so sweet to me, China. I love you."

As Zaire's words sunk into her brain, China fought the urge to cry. Although he'd told her he loved her before and she'd told him the same, each time one of them spoke the words it made her sorrowful. Neither of them could lose sight of her imminent departure. It would be foolish. *I'm here now*, she thought, pulling his head down, kissing him like she couldn't get enough of his delicious mouth.

As Zaire's tongue flicked in and out of her ear, China felt herself coming unglued. She couldn't wait to welcome the release. Then she quickly switched gears, hoping he'd never stop making love to her. What he gave to her was pure and true. He gave himself to her, all of him. What they had *was* very real, as real as it could get. What she planned to do about the authenticity of their love for each other had yet to be decided.

"China," he cried out loudly, "China, I love you… I can't hold back any longer. I'm losing it, baby…"

China felt every inch of Zaire's manhood jerking and pulsating inside her. Concentrating on the erotic trembling of her own body, she climaxed at the same moment he did, crying out his name as loudly as he cried hers.

Silent as nightfall, China and Zaire lay there, holding each other tightly. Neither was capable of an encore. Their breathing was under control, but she felt completely worn out and so did he. Sweat rolled from their bodies, but neither had enough strength to get out of bed to shower.

Zaire turned slightly and laid his head between China's breasts. Her body felt feverish to the touch. His body burned as hot as hers. He looked up at her. "You should be arrested."

China gave a weak laugh. "For what, Zaire?"

"For stealing my heart and invading my spirit. You're wicked, but I guess you already know that about yourself. I love the wickedness in you."

"Just as I love the quiet strength you possess. You're a thief, too. You stole my heart, and I got a feeling you don't plan to give it back. Am I right?"

"As right as rain! We can share hearts, but I won't ever give yours back."

China could barely find enough strength to smile, but she managed one. "I was worried about that. Why won't you give it back?"

He laid the back of his hand against her flushed cheek. "I plan to hold on to it for safekeeping. If I keep it in my possession, no one else can take it from you and break it. Trust me with your heart. I promise to cherish it."

"I trust you," she said drowsily. "I trust you with everything in me…"

Burying his face against her breasts, Zaire began crying. His entire body was racked with the pain he'd held inside for so long. "I know…you're leaving…in a week," he stammered, "yet there's so much unsaid. There are things I want to tell you but I can't seem to find the right words. Please be patient. It'll come."

Wondering what was at the crux of his agony and uncertainty, China held him tightly, gently touching his face, massaging his arms. Once again she wondered about who'd hurt him. "You can tell me anything, Zaire. I won't judge you one way or the other. Please tell me why you're so distraught. Does loving me hurt you?"

He raised his head until their eyes connected. Zaire didn't even bother to wipe away the tears. "China, there is so much going on inside me. I watched my mother abused day in and day out and did nothing about it. We all feared

Macon because we believed him capable of killing us in one of his drunken rages. I know I'm not the type of man who'd strike a woman. I'd cut my hand off first, before I hit someone I professed to love or anyone else."

"I know you're not that kind of man, Zaire. I'm glad you know it. Abuse is not hereditary, though some abusers want to make it so. Rage comes from many sources. Alcohol and drugs aren't the only reasons for an abuser's pain."

"That you know who I am as a man is important to me." He paused for a second. "I need to be sure I didn't put you on the spot when I asked to visit L.A. Do you want our relationship to continue, China? Or did I catch you off guard with the question?"

China took a moment to ponder her response. Pressing her lips into his forehead, she held them there for several seconds. Finally, she looked him right in the eye. "Zaire, I spoke my true feelings to your question. I didn't feel caught off guard or put on the spot. There's a big hurdle ahead of us, but we can't possibly leap over it if we don't try. I honestly don't know our future. But I do know I love you."

Zaire sighed. "Neither of us can know the future. But life won't be the same for me once you leave. I'll go back to doing what I love to do, but not as passionately as before. Work will keep me busy but it won't keep my mind off you. My family is capable of running this ranch without me if it ever comes to that."

China desired the same thing he did and thought it could work, but she couldn't let him tear himself away from his roots. This ranch had been his only woman for so long, and he was married to it. "I want you to visit me and I'll come here. When we're apart there are so many ways to stay connected—phones, e-mail, Skype. If we want more, I can consider looking for a nursing position in Brownsville.

There is a shortage in nursing across the nation. I want to give us my best shot."

"We'll both give our best." Turning over to lie flat on his back, he brought her into his arms and kissed her passionately.

China lay very still in his arms. Her body was tired yet her mind was racing. Never in her wildest imagination did she think she'd find true love on a dude ranch in Texas. But it had occurred, and there wasn't anything she could do about it. In her heart of hearts she desperately wanted to see him again. Otherwise she might be throwing away a lifetime of love and happiness. She didn't doubt their love was sincere. Sleep suddenly crept in to claim China, causing her to surrender. Zaire succumbed only minutes later.

Scooping up China into his arms, Zaire carried her into the bathroom, placing her into a hot bubble bath. The minute her body hit the water, she completely awakened. "Zaire, what're you doing?"

He grinned. "In your sleep you mentioned needing a bath. I decided to shower first and then run you a bath. We can have breakfast in the hotel restaurant before checking out." He looked at his watch. "It's already ten-thirty."

The bubble bath on her hands kept her from rubbing her eyes. "I can't believe the time. I must've been knocked out cold. How long have you been awake?"

"Long enough to shower and dress and pack the car. I didn't have the heart to wake you. You were sleeping like a log."

Kneeling down beside the tub, he took hold of the washcloth. Dipping it in the water, he let it run water over her shoulders and down over her breasts. All China could do was smile and relax. As he lathered the cloth with liquid soap, she braced herself for whatever he had in mind. Tenderly, he washed her body. "Does it feel good?"

China closed her eyes. "Better than good. If you weren't dressed already, I'd ask you to get in here with me."

Draping the cloth across her breasts, he wiped his hands on a towel and began stripping. "Anytime you want something, don't hesitate to ask. I can either deliver or I can't. Taking a bath with you is my pleasure, but we may have to get breakfast once we're on the road."

"Not a problem." She drew up her legs so he could get into the tub, making sure he had enough room. She stretched her legs back out once he was comfortable. Taking the washcloth away from her breasts, she poured more liquid soap onto it. After cleaning in between each of his toes, she scrubbed the soles of his feet. Outside of patients and her father, she'd never enjoyed washing anyone's feet so much. It was kind of erotic.

Reaching for China's hands, Zaire pulled her forward. Once she was close enough to him, he lifted her and settled her down onto his lap. "I bet there's something exciting about making love in the tub. Want to try it out?" His eyes glimmered with childish mischief. "I'd sure like to."

Throwing her head back, China howled. "You *are* a bad boy, aren't you?" It took her a second to get in a position to lower herself onto his ramrod-stiff erection. "Let's see just how bad a boy you can be."

"Girl, I'm not sure you really want to know, but I'm willing to give you some idea." Moving his head forward, he captured her lips with his. He then drew back, only to claim her mouth again. "I love kissing you."

China outlined his lips with the tip of her tongue. "I also like kissing you. Sometimes it takes you too long to kiss me."

"From now on, I promise to kiss you as soon as I see you…"

Silencing Zaire, China seared her lips onto his, deeply probing his mouth with her tongue. Hungrily, wildly, she kissed him passionately. Lifting herself, she slid down over his manhood, connecting him to the hot, moist opening of her flower.

Throwing back her head, China gasped wantonly. The sheer pleasure of having Zaire inside her had China out of her mind with desire. She was hotter than she'd ever been for him. Eager to have him fulfill her physical needs and douse the flames burning an inferno between her legs, she moved up and down on his sex. "Does it feel good?" she asked, recalling the same question from him.

"Words to explain how good it feels elude me. Love me, China. Love me like you've lost total control. Love me the way you'd want me to love you."

Fifteen minutes after Zaire pulled out of the valet lane, China looked over at him. "I've had a wonderful time. Thank you for making my first week so special. I hope the second week will be just as eventful."

"You're welcome, China. I plan to outdo myself during the rest of your stay."

Zaire kept his eyes on the road. He'd planned to tell China his past history with one woman in particular, and he knew that waiting until he knew their future wasn't fair to her. He made a silent vow to tell her everything before she left the ranch.

A huge smile was on China's tanned face. Waving at Zaire from the front door of the cabin, she inserted the key and turned the lock. Entering, she carried her belongings inside and made her way to the bedroom. After removing clothing from her bag, she tossed everything but her swim-suit into the dirty clothes hamper. Because her swimwear smelled like the sea, she hung it up on the metal bar in the bedroom to wash later.

A glance at the clock let her know Zaire had made good time in getting back to the ranch. Time had flown by. She smiled. That's how it was with them. Time sprouted wings whenever they were together.

Knowing she was meeting Zaire for dinner, she hurried and put all her belongings back in place so she could lie down and rest. After eating they planned to take a ride out to their favorite lake by the old oak tree. A barbecue and dance were taking place tonight in the main pavilion. Since her favorite band was the main attraction, she looked forward to the evening's festivities.

The cabin phone rang and China rushed across the room to answer it. "Hello," she cheerfully greeted.

"Hey, China, it's Gayle. Zaire popped into the dining hall a few minutes ago, so I knew you guys were back. How was the trip?"

"Fantastic! South Padre Island is beautiful. The only problem was the lack of time. I could've stayed there an entire week…and I'd probably still dread leaving. Zaire is something else. He's so romantic."

Several seconds of silence ensued.

"Gayle, are you still there?"

"I was just thinking." Gayle sounded cautious.

"What's wrong, Gayle? Your voice changed. What're you thinking?" Fearful of what she might hear, China plopped down on the bed to listen intently.

"I'm sorry, China. It's just that I'm thinking about Zaire. Has he told you he's in love with you?"

China's eyes blinked hard, wondering if this had any-thing to do with Zaire's romantic past. "As a matter of fact, he has. What's that have to do with you? Do you think I'd hurt him?"

"Not wittingly, but Zaire *will* get hurt. When you leave next week, he'll be utterly devastated. He's so in love with you."

"And I'm in love with him. What're you saying? What's expected of me?"

"We don't want you to give him any false hopes. He's sensitive. Dealing with women isn't a regular occurrence for him. Zaire buries himself in his work. He's been hurt before and trust is a big problem for him."

"He shared his trust issues with me. Who is the woman that hurt him?"

"He'll have to share that, but I'll say this much. Zaire was hurt badly."

Feeling sick inside, China put a hand to her stomach. "And you think I'm capable of tearing apart his heart? Who else thinks I'd hurt Zaire?"

"No one thinks you'll hurt him intentionally. This ranch is his pot of gold at the rainbow's end. He'd try to live in L.A. if you asked him to, but he wouldn't be happy. The relationship would suffer under extreme pressure. Try and understand what I'm saying. I believe he's torn between making you happy and living on the ranch."

"Gayle, I'm not in the habit of inviting outside interference into my life. Zaire and I will work through our issues without assistance from anyone else."

"I don't know any other way to express our concerns. The family doesn't want Zaire devastated. Ms. Bernice believes you love him and that you'd never hurt him. She doesn't think you've come to grips with your emotions, but that love will end up the victor anyway. She's an eternal optimist. Mr. Cobb and the aunts believe the same as she does. Are they right, China? Are you incapable of breaking Zaire's heart?"

Refusing to respond to such a heartless query, China tamped down her anger. "I've already said how I feel. Zaire's feelings are what matters to me."

"Suit yourself, but his past hurt will rear its ugly head."

"If it does pose a threat, Zaire and I will handle it together."

"If it's any comfort, I know you love Zaire. Take time to think it all through. I'm happy we met you. And there's not one of us who isn't rooting for you two. I'll see you tonight at the pavilion. Zaire mentioned you'd be joining us."

"I'll be there, Gayle. I'm looking forward to seeing everyone," China fibbed. With a heavy heart, China hung up the phone.

China wondered if city life versus country living *wasn't* her dilemma. Maybe her love for Zaire could overcome anything. But in the next second, her mind told her to run for her life. It was up to her to listen to her mind or fulfill the desires of her heart.

Stretching out on the bed, China thought about everything Gayle had said. Then she went back over the numerous conversations she and Zaire had had during her stay. She'd been open and honest with him about everything. She wanted them to have a real shot at happiness, just like he said he did.

Why hadn't he discussed his broken relationship? He'd mentioned his pain, but what little else he'd said wasn't sitting well with her. If it was still too painful for Zaire to talk about, perhaps he wasn't over it.

She planned to confront him about his past history. If they were to bare all, he had to be a participant. Trying not to worry about what might happen later, she closed her eyes.

* * *

Just as Zaire had promised, he kissed China the moment he saw her. "You look hot!" His eyes roved her body. Clad in all-black Western gear with rhinestones on her denim vest, she looked like a real Texas cowgirl. Zaire pulled her to him. "There's something missing. Ah," he said, "I know just what it is. Stay there. I'll be right back." He took off running.

Puzzled by what he was up to, China sat down to await his return. Her love for him brimmed over in her heart, but her fears were strong. City living would kill his spirit. She was sure of it.

If any major sacrifices were made, she'd be the one to take them on. Instead of living on the ranch, she'd already thought about getting an apartment in Brownsville. She and Zaire should have some distance while they got to know each other even better. Living on the ranch would make things too convenient. Both had to be satisfied with their living conditions. Brownsville was a thriving city. She'd researched the city's hospitals on her laptop and they were all hiring nurses.

Many medical facilities allowed résumés to be submitted electronically. Hers was stored on her hard drive and she'd sent out several already. She planned to go into the city to visit a few facilities to get a feel. Her work history was stellar.

Zaire popped back into the cabin, interrupting her thoughts. Bringing his hands from behind his back, he presented her with one of the most beautiful black Stetsons she'd ever seen. The hatband was a double row of rhinestones, perfectly matching her outfit.

Getting to her feet, China moved close to him. "Put my Stetson on for me. I want to see if you really know how big my head is."

Zaire set the hat atop her head. "It's a perfect fit. I measured your big head just right. I've got another present for you. I peeked at your shoe size when you weren't around. We'll go to Brownsville to pick up your custom-made boots. You'll love them."

China squealed. "I can hardly wait! Are they fancy?"

"They're one of a kind. I designed them. I've got lots of unrevealed skills."

She kissed him gently on the mouth. "I don't know if I can stand any more of your skills."

Zaire grinned, sticking out his broad chest. "The hat looks super on you. You'll be the belle of the ball. Let's get this show on the road."

"I'm ready, Zaire. I can't wait to show off my new headgear. Thanks for the Stetson. Boots will make me an official Texan."

"You already have Texas blood. Mr. B. is a native Texan. He loved this state."

China's eyes filled with tears. "He did. I'm so sorry he didn't get back here to live his retirement out. Leaving me behind was a big problem for him."

"I know how he felt. I don't want to leave you behind either, and I don't want you to leave me. We're going to make this work."

"Maybe we can commute and have the best of both worlds," China said.

"Whatever we have to do to be together, we'll do it, China."

"I love you so much, Zaire." Hoping he'd feel her love flowing from her heart into his, she kissed him ardently.

The entire Kingdom family was seated at the reserved tables. With all eyes on her, this was the first time China felt like an outsider. This family had high expectations. If she failed them, their disappointment in her would be massive. *Don't worry about failing them,* she quietly told herself. *The two of us have to be my main concern. No one else has to live for us or with us. This is between no one but Zaire and me.*

Bernice was the first one out of her seat, opening her arms to China. "Hello, sweetheart! You look more and more like a Texan every time I see you. Honey," she whispered into China's ear, "don't listen to anything but your heart. Don't allow anyone to bully you. I've already told Gayle to mind her business. She doesn't speak for our family. We've got your back. Now come sit down and join the fun."

The aunts also gave China hugs and more encouraging words. Their comments pretty much mirrored Bernice's. China was pleased by the way they'd received her so warmly. Relief flooded her. Ms. Bernice and her sisters helped muster her courage. As Zaire led her to the table, Zurich, Zane and Mr. Cobb greeted her with big hugs. Gayle only smiled, nodding in China's direction, appearing none too happy.

"Forgive me for not getting up," Hailey said, rubbing her stomach. "I might not be able to wedge back in here if I move. It's good to see you, China. You're looking fit and tan. Looks like the sun gravitated to you. You're a bronzed beauty."

Slinging his arm around China in a possessive way, Zaire wanted his family to know he was madly in love. The music was blaring. Without waiting for others to hit the dance floor, Zaire took her hand. "Let's get the party started. Is anyone else coming?"

As though the aunts had been waiting on an invite, they excitedly began to file out of the opposite booth. Bernice and Morgan joined them as did Zane and Gayle. Zurich and Hailey planned to sit the night out since she was close to her due date.

A slow song was on by the time the group made it to the floor. That didn't stop the sisters from forming a circle. Holding hands, they moved with the tempo.

Zaire brought China in close to his body. Resting his chin atop her head, he began dancing. She loved how smoothly he executed his steps and she easily stayed right with him. She felt they were excellent dance partners. She recalled having two left feet as a teenager. Slow dancing had been harder for her than fast dances.

He put his mouth to her ear. "Get enough rest?"

"Not as much as I would've liked, but I'm okay."

China hadn't been able to shut off her mind after Gayle's unexpected call. She had repeatedly mulled over the conversation. Gayle had had a lot of nerve getting into their personal business. China didn't hold grudges, but she wouldn't take it too kindly if it happened again.

Bernice was right. Their love affair wasn't anyone else's business.

Chapter 12

Outside in the parking lot, appearing shocked and amazed, China watched Zaire insert a silver key into the ignition of a beautifully painted motorcycle.

"We're going to take this chariot." Removing one of the helmets from the back, he handed it to her.

China swallowed hard. "I've never rode on a motorcycle. It looks intimidating, just like your huge horses." A resigned look settled in her eyes. "Oh, well, nothing ventured, nothing gained. How did this bike get here?"

"Zurich parked it for me. This is everyday stuff to us. We're always there for each other." He gave her a helmet, snapping the chin strap in place. "This is what I need you to do. Whenever I turn the bike, lean with me. The oak tree isn't far, but we'll encounter a couple of sharp bends. Sure you're okay about riding?"

China shrugged. "I believe I can handle it. If I can't, can I cause trouble?"

"You'll be fine. As you feel the bike turning, just lean. It's not that big of a deal. It's easier than learning to ride a horse."

"I guess." China stood by, watching as Zaire took off his hat and put on his helmet. "If I like the bike, will you teach me how to ride it?"

Chuckling, Zaire helped China mount. "I don't know. I've never taught anyone to ride a motorcycle. Zurich had me riding before I was fifteen. I'll give it some thought. Remember to hold on tight to me."

"No problem with that. I love holding on to you," she flirted, smiling.

Zaire revved the engine until it roared. "Here we go." Taking off slowly through the parking lot, he sped up once he reached the road. With China's hands digging into his waist, he was sure she wouldn't let go.

Feeling exhilarated, loving the feel of the wind rushing by, China's eyes were wide and bright. She nestled her head against Zaire's back. Continuing to hold on tightly, she grew more and more excited. If not for the helmet, she'd love to feel the wind swooshing through her hair. She wished he'd go faster but she knew better than to ask. He was a safety guy and he wouldn't do anything reckless to put them in danger.

In less than twenty minutes, Zaire parked the bike on the grass. Cutting the engine, he got off. While assisting China's dismount, he was moved by the sparkle in her eyes. "How was it for you, babe?"

Jumping up and down, grinning, she clapped her hands. "Loved it! You really do know how to live a free and easy life. I want what you have so much of. You're at peace with yourself."

Removing a blanket from a sidesaddle bag, Zaire took China's hand and climbed the grassy knoll leading to the great oak. Spreading the blanket under the tree, he lowered himself to the ground and drew her down onto his lap. "Glad you enjoyed the ride. I *am* at peace with myself, most of the time. It hasn't always been that way. There's something I need to say. Will you hear me out?"

China nodded. "Of course I will."

Zaire tenderly wrapped his arms around her. "I was once romantically involved. I thought I was in love. Until I met you, I believed it wholeheartedly. What I feel with you and for you is totally different from any past experience. I'm happy I'm single. Otherwise, I couldn't have gotten this close to you."

China made direct eye contact. "Is it possible your feelings are confused? Maybe what you felt before was true love and not what you're feeling now. Can that be?"

"No, no, China, I know the difference…and it's a big one. I'm more relaxed around you and much happier. What I feel for you is nothing like anything I've felt before. Anyhow, I thought my heart was broken. I never told a soul how relieved I was at being left in the dust. It wouldn't have worked with us. If she hadn't left when she did, she would've escaped sooner or later."

Zaire still hadn't mentioned the lady's name, China noted. "Who was she? What's her name?"

"There's no importance in it, but her name was Charmaine Colton. We were engaged to be married. A wedding never took place."

"I'm sorry for any pain you experienced. You don't deserve to be hurt. That's why I want us to be sure. I'm thinking of taking an apartment in Brownsville until we get to know each other inside and out. I don't want to live out here, because it's just too convenient for us. We might need space, so as not to get on each other's nerves. I need to find a nursing job and I don't know what type of shifts I may get. I want to see you and get settled at the same time. What do you think?"

"Good idea. Brownsville isn't L.A., but it has a great city life. South Padre's only a short distance away and you already know how it is there. I want what you do. If it's to live in L.A., I'm willing to relocate."

Moved by Zaire's thoughtfulness, China shook her head from side to side. "I won't ask you to leave Texas. This ranch is your baby. You helped birth the land and you continue to nurture it. You've made so many expansion plans. Your family is here. It's only me in L.A. Asking you to leave all of this wonder isn't in me. We either work it out here or we don't do it period."

Zaire's eyebrows lifted. "That's a strong statement, don't you think?"

Lowering her head, she riveted her mouth to his, giving him a staggering kiss and leaving him reeling. "Now that's a strong statement. I've already made up my mind about how I want us to do this. You know how strong willed I am."

"I've definitely run into your sheer determination. When would you be able to move this way?"

"It'll take at least a couple months to get it done. Landing a job here is a must before I resign my current position. I don't want to sell my father's house so I need to lease it. It's a lovely place, filled with memories."

"Keep it ready and available. We can fly there whenever you miss home. I can find a property management company to handle it. Like you said, we can commute and have the best of both worlds."

"A house unattended will invite vandalism. I'm sure there's a loving family who needs a nice place to live. I have to decide what to do with my father's Texas land. I haven't seen it yet. I brought the deed in case I got a chance."

"We'll make it happen. I'll look at the deed to see how far it is from here. From what I recall Mr. B. saying, it's nearby."

"I think you're right." Moving from Zaire's lap, she stretched out on the blanket. A crook of her finger summoned him to join her.

Lying alongside her, Zaire lowered his head, kissing her breathless. A light breeze was blowing, making it a beautiful night for lovemaking under the stars.

Zaire tugged loose China's vest. After undoing several buttons on her shirt, Zaire's hand reached inside and tenderly cupped a firm breast. Freeing her warm flesh from the bra, he bent his head and suckled. As his other hand stroked China through her jeans, she felt the fiery friction tampering with her sanity.

Sexual tension getting to her in the worst way, China reached for his belt. The Western-style buckle was big but easy to release. Instead of trying to remove the wide strip of leather, she simply let down his zipper. Sticking her small hand inside the opening, she found his erection. Massaging his hardened flesh, she unleashed her tongue on his inner ear.

Following China's lead, he lowered her zipper and removed her jeans. Zaire stripped away his jeans next. Inching his way inside her, slowly and tantalizingly, he gently manipulated her sweet flesh.

Wrapping her legs around Zaire's waist, she afforded him easy access. As he slid deeper into her, the moaning and groaning began. Stroking his buttocks, she whimpered against his ear. Beneath him, she raised her hips to welcome each grind and fiery thrust. Her fingernails found his back, gently scraping up and down his spine. She was moving under him like a wild tigress.

Losing himself to China's feral urgings, pumping harder

and faster, he caused her moisture to flow like white-hot lava. Lifting himself off her, positioning his body along-side hers again, Zaire used his fingers to spread open her flower.

Dipping his head downward, Zaire's tongue laved her tenderly. Feeling an explosion rocking her inner chamber, he reentered her, urgently pumping his way into a mindless haze of ecstasy. With his body trembling all over, Zaire's powerful release made him wish this mind-blowing feeling would never cease.

Rolling onto his back, Zaire easily lifted China and brought her to rest atop him. "I don't know about us. We're maniacs for each other." He covered her face with whisper soft kisses. "This isn't just about sex for me. I've said it before. I make love to you, China, because I love you deeply."

She kissed his nose and forehead. "Your feelings show. There are so many things for us to get straight…and I'm very optimistic." She yawned. "I'm bone tired and I could fall asleep right here."

Pulling the blanket up around them, Zaire brought her head to his chest. "Go to sleep. Listen to the lake as it sings you a lullaby. I'll wake you in a little while."

"I'd rather dress and go back to the cabin and shower. I'll be ready to climb into bed. Can we stay together tonight?"

Zaire smiled tenderly. "I want that."

"It would've been hard sleeping without you next to me."

"It's an alluring thought, China. I hope it stays that way."

Freshly showered, smelling of jasmine and cherry blossom, China was already settled in bed. Zaire was in the kitchen brewing tea to help them relax. She was more wound down than he knew and had propped herself up in bed. Once her head hit the pillow, it'd be all over.

As China's mind gravitated toward what Zaire had told her about his broken engagement she was happy he'd given the woman a name. The thought brought her and Gayle's conversation back to mind.

Gayle had definitely made her feelings known to the rest of the Kingdom family. China liked Gayle, but she wouldn't hesitate to put her in her place. If it came to that, she'd practice discretion and rebuff anger. It wouldn't do any good to go off the deep end if she was again forced to tell Zane's girlfriend to mind her own business. China wondered if Zaire knew about what had transpired between them. She doubted it. He would've handled Gayle by now.

Zaire walked into the bedroom, carrying a tray. China's eyes fell softly on his sexy body. Wearing only a towel, his bulging abs and pectorals made her shudder.

She loved the wide expanse of his chest and the comfort she felt laying her head there.

If China never saw Zaire again, God forbid, she wouldn't be able to forget those strapping thighs, washboard abs and strong arms. *Who was she trying to kid?* China wouldn't ever forget a single thing about him.

Setting down the tray on the dresser top, Zaire picked up a hot mug of cinnamon tea and handed it to China. "Be careful. It's piping hot."

"Just the way I like my man," she flirted.

Once China had a firm hold of the mug, he went back for his. Strolling back to bed, he removed a coaster from a stack on the nightstand and put down his cup. Climbing into bed, he positioned himself upright, settling next to the woman he couldn't get enough of. "This is cozy and I love it. I can't ask for more than a sexy woman, candlelight and hot tea. Did your shower relax you?"

China nodded. "That's why I'm sitting up in bed. If I'd laid my head on a pillow, I'd be out like a light."

"Drink your tea, scoot down in bed and let Mr. Sandman have his way. I won't keep you awake."

She grew quiet and thoughtful. "Is there a reason you didn't share your bad breakup with me earlier? I wonder why you kept it a secret when everyone else knows."

Zaire eyed China openly. "Who knows? Who are you talking to? Are you grilling my family about me? I hope not. I wouldn't like it or appreciate it."

Feeling affronted, China looked down her nose at Zaire. "Oh, no, I know you didn't go there! Why do you think I'd ask anyone about your private affairs? And why are you so sensitive about my curiosity?"

Unable to explain why her curiosity bothered him, Zaire stared hard at her. "I thought I'd satisfied your curiosity. I get a feeling you know more about my past affair than you're saying. Did you already know about Charmaine when I mentioned her?"

"Gayle told me, but she didn't give a name." Wishing she hadn't let the cat out of the bag, China bit down on her lower lip. *Oh, God, what have I said and done?*

"Gayle? Why would you ask her about my relationships in the first place?"

Anger flashed white-hot in China's eyes. "For your information, I didn't ask her a damn thing." No longer caring that she hadn't protected Gayle's involvement, she glared at Zaire. "Furthermore, she called to give me a so-called friendly warning, saying she was thinking of you, not wanting you to get hurt again. Isn't tending to Zane enough to keep her busy? Why is she suddenly up in our business?"

Both angry and mortified by what he'd just heard, Zaire slid out of bed. Walking over to the chair, he grabbed his underwear and jeans and dressed hastily. "We'll talk later, China."

"Wait a minute," China shouted, "where are you going? You're upset with me, and I'm not guilty of a thing."

"Sorry if I falsely accused you." He looked at the clock. "I've got to settle this tonight. Everyone's probably still at the pavilion. Gayle can't go sticking her nose into my business. She hasn't said a word to me about any of this. I fight my own battles, vigorously."

Leaping out of bed, China ran over to Zaire. "Please don't do this. It'll only blow up in my face. Gayle will hate me."

"She should've thought of that before overstepping boundaries. Zane won't be happy, either. She knew how he'd feel. This isn't the first time she's stuck her nose where it doesn't belong." Zaire turned on his heels.

"Wait," she screamed, "I'm going with you. We should confront this together."

"You stay right here! That's my final word. I've got this. Believe me, I've got it!" Zaire stormed out, all but slamming the front door off its hinges.

China was frantic. This shouldn't have happened. Zaire was furious.

Scrambling back across the room, China opened a nightstand drawer, pulling out a laminated list of important phone numbers. Locating the pavilion extension, she dialed it in haste. No answer. Remembering she had Gayle's home and cell numbers stored in her cell, she grabbed up her purse, practically ripping the zipper apart to get to the phone.

Right after the voice mail picked up, China bitterly conceded defeat. She wasn't going to reach Gayle by phone or text messaging. Her only way to see Gayle was at the pavilion. While retrieving her clothes, Zaire's matter-of-fact remarks echoed in her ear.

"You stay right here."

It was obvious Zaire didn't want her involved in whatever he had to say to Gayle. She grimaced, hating what she may've caused.

Without looking back at his family, Zaire angrily exited the pavilion. Gayle had his blood boiling, but he'd firmly put her in her place. Wondering if he should go back to China or head home, he decided it wasn't fair to leave her hanging. Zaire desperately wanted to see her and apologize.

Pounding on China's cabin door proved futile. Zaire couldn't help wondering where she was. Then it dawned on him that she probably didn't want to see him. He had handled everything badly. How was he to make it up to her? Zaire had no problem admitting he had been dead wrong, but would she listen? Having it out with Gayle and setting her straight had taken precedence over making things right with China.

Stretched out on top of his king mattress, biding time until he had to do some work, Zaire looked up at the ceiling, tears threatening. Fearing that he'd totally blown it with China, his body ached. He couldn't deny he loved her. Hopefully she'd love him despite everything, despite his fears. He had a lot to consider.

Rolling over and posting up on his side, Zaire snatched up the jangling telephone receiver. "Zaire here," he greeted blandly.

"Hailey is in labor," Bernice said anxiously. "The contractions aren't close enough together to head to the hospital. She wants to wait as long as she can. Zurich is with her. I'll keep you informed, Zaire."

"I'll wait to hear back. Call as soon as you know more. Talk to you then, Mom." Cradling the phone, he leapt off the bed only to pick up the receiver again. His heart pounding uncontrollably, he dialed cabin nine and waited impatiently for a response. But there was no answer.

He headed toward the front door. The thought of Hailey in labor made him smile, yet he felt apprehensive. The Kingdoms would soon have a newcomer in the family. Happy for both Zurich and Hailey, Zaire closed his eyes and dispensed with his troubling thoughts. His quiet supplication was for a healthy newborn.

Surprised to see Gayle at her cabin door, China took two steps back. The visitor stood stock-still. "Are you coming in, Gayle?"

Gayle posted a hand on her hip. "I don't have to come in to speak my mind. When I spoke to you about Zaire, it was out of concern. I had no idea you're a snitch. I didn't think you'd go spill your guts to Zaire."

China glared at Gayle. "Now you hear what I think. The things you said were inappropriate, but I swallowed them whole. Zaire is a strong man. He doesn't need anyone to speak for him, Gayle. As for what you think about me, I don't care. Know this. Zaire and I are planning a life together. Your input isn't needed or wanted."

"Listen, you have no idea—"

China held up her hand in a halting position. "You've said enough already—and I don't want to hear more." No longer in control of her anger, China slammed the door in Gayle's face, regretting it instantly. Yet she didn't see any good in reopening it to apologize. Gayle had a declaration of war in her eyes and China wasn't about to enter into another battle.

Gayle pounded hard on the door. "I'm not finished, China. You need to open up and listen."

"Gayle, go away. I'm sure Zane wouldn't like this. I have no quarrel with you. You need to leave Zaire and me alone."

"I've known Zaire a lot longer than you. If he doesn't know what's good for him, I do. How do you come up in here and steal my thunder? I'm not having it. I've been around the Kingdom family a long time."

Gayle's last two statements brought it home to roost for China. Gayle was jealous of her and probably feared China and Zaire might make it to the altar before her and Zane. She saw China as an intrusion in the family Gayle had yet to become a part of. Her motives were crystal clear.

"If you want to come in, I'll listen to you, Gayle. But you're not yelling at me from out there. What's it going to be?"

"Just open the damn door, China."

Ignoring Gayle's rude demand, China walked away from the door, only to turn around and snatch it open. "Listen, you, I meant what I said about the yelling. Talk calmly or get the hell off my doorstep."

Pushing her way inside, Gayle dropped her purse on the floor and plopped her butt down on the sofa. Looking back at China, she seethed, waiting for her to take a seat.

China slowly took a chair. "I'm all ears, Gayle. Please make it quick."

Gayle sighed hard. "I resent the way you've forced yourself on my family…"

"Your family!" China was outraged. "Excuse me. Is your last name Kingdom? Are you suddenly engaged to one?"

Gayle's eyes narrowed to tiny slits. "It'll happen. We've been exclusive for three years. We've talked marriage, but Zane hasn't actually proposed. He will, though." Gayle looked like she was ready to cry. "You haven't been around but a minute, yet Zaire's ready to trek down the aisle. You're ruining my plans."

China appeared puzzled. "What plans?"

"Marry Zane and live happily ever after. The special attention paid to us by his family has been transplanted to you and Zaire. It's not fair. They're all gushing over you, as if you're a precious crown jewel. It's China this, China that."

Feeling terribly sorry for Gayle, China wanted to hug her, but she knew it wouldn't be well received. "I didn't come here to fall in love with a Kingdom man. I'm not in your way. The Kingdom family hasn't transferred attention or love from you and Zane to Zaire and me. I'm sorry you feel this way."

Gayle got to her feet. "I don't believe you. I think you're selfish and you'll eventually destroy Zaire." Standing, Gayle stormed toward the exit. She turned and leveled an angry scowl at China. "If you're smart, you'll stay the hell out of my way."

China could hardly believe her ears. The look in Gayle's eyes was deadly. How had it come down to this with Zane's girlfriend? China had no idea. Zaire's attempt to get Gayle to mind her own business had apparently run amok. China knew it was futile to bring to Zaire's attention this latest episode of *Gayle Gone Crazy.*

Chapter 13

Sobbing uncontrollably, China's hands shook as she tried to get a grip on her emotions. Finding out that Zaire had assigned a ranch hand to handle the riding lesson, she'd returned to the cabin, bitterly disappointed. It was obvious he didn't want to see her. He was probably still seething with anger from the last encounter.

Whatever Zaire had said to Gayle obviously hadn't had any impact. Perhaps she had lied to him like she'd done to China. China found it hard to believe Zaire would entertain Gayle's lies, yet there wasn't another explanation for him avoiding her.

Was it over? Should she just try to accept it, no matter how hard it was?

China wasn't completely convinced that Zaire was done with her. She'd written a letter to let him know how much she loved him. Writing down her feelings was more of a way to get her emotions outside her than anything else.

In the penned note she'd told him she'd be there if he ever changed his mind about giving them a chance. There was nothing she wanted more than to be with him. Since Zaire hadn't called her, she'd made up her mind to leave Whispering Lakes Ranch. She didn't want to go. China wanted desperately to stay and convince Zaire of how sincere she was about seeing if they had a future.

Packing her things was difficult. Departing from a ranch she'd fallen in love with was no easy feat. Six days of vacation were left, but she didn't feel encouraged to stay. Thoughts of leaving behind the man she madly loved stripped her soul bare.

Zaire Kingdom was the only man China had fallen head over heels in love with, the only heartthrob she'd ever truly love. Her heart belonged to him. It might be difficult to sacrifice her life in California, but she was willing to do it.

The career China had worked her tail off for was a burning passion, just as working the ranch was Zaire's. She loved nursing, and he loved owning and running Whispering Lakes Ranch. Thank God she was in a worldwide profession. Zaire was a bit more limited in his career as a rancher, but he was also a gifted architect.

Zaire could no more live permanently in the city than China had once believed she could live out the rest of her life in the country, no matter how beautiful it was. Perhaps she was wrong about him. She'd done an about-face. Dividing time between both places was even an option, but a lot of hours would burn up in travel. The ranch was Zaire's livelihood, garnering way more than adequate revenue. Whispering Lakes was his conception, his first love.

China loved Zaire too much to even think of asking him to consider living elsewhere. She believed he loved her enough to try L.A., but she didn't want to put him in a position to choose. She could only imagine the chaos they'd both endure if he ended up making wrong choices. Ranching fit his persona to a tee.

China saw firsthand how much Zaire loved his life. She'd seen him hard at work, and he'd finally begun to play and enjoy it. Any woman who loved and respected her man wouldn't make unreasonable and purely selfish demands of him. Asking a Texas cowboy to move to a metropolis was downright unfair.

Zaire's home was on the ranch, where his people were. Because she longed for a family just like his, it was next to impossible to ask him to go. The Kingdoms loved each other. She was willing to make any necessary adjustments, but it looked like Zaire had turned to a different page.

Why else hadn't he called or come by?

Removing intimate apparel from the chest of drawers, she carelessly tossed them into the suitcase on top of other clothing. Toiletries would get packed last since she planned to shower before hitting the road. Looking at the clock, she saw it was getting late. If Zaire didn't call within the next hour or so, she was out.

If China stayed, she feared making matters worse. It was so unlike Zaire to get mad and stay mad. Hours had passed since she'd last seen him.

A tap on her shoulder made China turn around. Zane standing behind her was startling. What brought him out to her cabin? "Hi." Her insides bubbled from a bad case of nerves. Hoping nothing had happened to Zaire or anyone else, China hid her fear. Perhaps Hailey had gone into labor. Maybe her nursing skills were needed. *Stop it,* she berated mentally. *Turn it off! Give Zane a chance to tell you why he's here.*

Zane eyed China curiously. "What's going on? I hope it's not what it looks like."

China rocked back on her heels. "What's that?"

"That you're sneaking out of here like a thief in the night. Does Zaire know you're leaving? Six days are left on your reservation."

"He doesn't know. I haven't heard from him since we had a blowup. Staying on the ranch will further complicate our relationship." She sighed deeply. "Zane, I love Zaire and was willing to change my life to be with him. It's obvious he no longer wants that. I love my job, the people and the city I live in. But I love Zaire more."

Zane scratched his head. "Then I don't see the problem."

"Last evening he said he was going to find Gayle and straighten out things with her. He never came back, nor has he phoned. I can easily interpret his actions."

Zane nodded. "He told Gayle to her face to stay out of his personal business." Zane's expression turned thoughtful. "I understand you loving your job and L.A., but do they make you feel like Zaire does? Can you go from day to day without my brother in your life? Is a city and a job capable of bringing you the ultimate satisfaction?"

Tears slid from China's eyes. "No. I had a full life before I came here, Zane. I have personal and professional obligations to tie up. Everything I lay claim to is in Los Angeles. And I can't claim someone who doesn't want me."

"Is any of this as important as you two committing yourselves to your love? I *know* you love him. He loves you. The family loves both. We've never seen two people more suited. Standards of living and addresses can be negotiated. True love can't."

"Zane, I wish I knew how to have it all. Can anyone have everything they desire? Besides, I don't think you've heard a thing I've said. Zaire *hasn't* made contact with me, not the other way around. I'm dying to hear from him."

"Zaire was angry last night. He told us all to butt out. I think you're wrong about him not wanting you, but it's just an opinion. At any rate, there's been enough meddling. Please stay until daylight. It's tricky getting off this ranch when you don't know it like the back of your hand."

"I beg to differ, Zane. I *do* know it, intimately. Zaire has taken me to every nook and cranny on these magnificent lands. I know it all right…and I know I'll never forget a single thing about it."

Reaching out for China, Zane brought her into his arms, hugging her gently. "It's a pleasure knowing you. You fit in around here perfectly. Zurich, Hailey, Gayle and I are extremely fond of you…and I believe you know how much Mom and Morgan have come to love you. You're also a huge hit with our aunts."

"I feel the exact same way about the Kingdoms. You've been wonderful. I especially love the bond your mother and I created. She's a warm, understanding woman. I pray she'll eventually learn the truth of what really happened."

China knew Zane was wrong about Gayle's fondness for her, but he'd have to find it out on his own. It wasn't up to her to tell him that his woman had set a trap for him.

"Out of the folks I mentioned, Zaire is the only one who has to love you unconditionally. He has the most to lose." Zane gulped hard. "Please make sure this is what you really want before you take off. Zaire has never given away his heart—and I got a hunch this is a first for you. Goodbye, Miss China Braxton." Zane kissed her forehead then turned to walk away.

China looked puzzled by Zane's remarks. "What about Charmaine?"

Zane stopped. Turning to face China, he shrugged.

"What about her? She was here and she left. Make no mistake about this, China. She didn't take Zaire's heart with her. I know my brother. He said he was in love but he wasn't. It's confirmed for me every time I see him with you. The way he is now compared to the way he was then… well, there *is* no comparison." Tipping his hat, he strode off. Zane had refrained from telling her about Hailey. He wanted China to stay out of her love for Zaire—and for no other reason.

Yet again, Zane walked back to China. "For what it's worth, Zaire *did* come back to you last night. The door wasn't answered. He assumed he wasn't welcome."

China opened her mouth to speak, but all she managed was to gulp in fresh air. The burning pain in her chest was excruciating. So she wasn't the only one who'd suffered devastation. Zaire was also in pain. Zane had given her a mind-changing fact. Leaving like this was wrong. She didn't know how to get through this goodbye. No matter if she stayed until they talked or left without doing so, good-byes were inevitable.

What if they could still part with a so long and see you real soon?

Standing stock-still, China watched Zane's truck disappear. *How had he known she was leaving early?* China knew for a fact she hadn't said a word to anyone about an early departure. Perhaps Zane had come there to say something different from what he'd said. When he'd seen her preparing for an unannounced getaway, maybe he'd switched gears. Regardless, Zane had said exactly what she needed to hear.

As China's car crept through the huge wrought-iron exit gates, she was unsuccessful in turning off her tears. Her eyes ran like water faucets. The pain in her heart was dagger sharp. A day had passed and Zaire not showing up or calling had her reverting to her original plan.

Once she was past the gate, China suddenly swerved the car onto the road's shoulder. Shifting into Park, she got out. Walking to the front of her vehicle, she leaned against its hood. Looking back on how and where she'd spent the most glorious days and passion-filled nights of her life, unforgettable memories began to rush her brain, crowding out coherence.

This was it. She was leaving. Zaire was staying. Misery and pain threatened to become permanent residents inside her heart.

Falling to her knees, pressing her hands hard into the dirt, China wished it was cement. Leaving her prints upon this land forever wouldn't necessarily make Zaire remember her, but it'd immortalize her presence.

"Will seeing my prints day in and day out be as painful for him as it'll be for me not to see him? God, that hurts so much!" China wished no ill will on the man she loved with every fiber of her being. All she wanted for him were wondrous things, a magnificent life—and a chance to live out his days on his beloved ranch.

China got back into the car. Blackness surrounded her. Riveted to the leather seat, she revisited the idea of staying to face Zaire. Confused and terribly upset, she suddenly felt winded. Fear crept back in.

There were consequences to every action, but she was determined to find out if she was a winner or a loser. "I have to go back. I have to be honest with Zaire, telling him exactly how I feel. He expects it from me, no less than what I expect from myself. I refuse to taint the beauty of our relationship."

China cranked the engine and turned the car back toward the gates. A couple of seconds later she couldn't believe what was happening. Either the gates were stuck or they wouldn't open for entry. Then she recalled Zaire pressing a remote above the sun visor of his SUV when they'd arrived late one night.

Resigning herself to calling for help, China knew Zane was her best bet, the only one with an inkling of what was happening. Removing her cell from its holder on the dash, she gasped. The device hadn't been plugged into a battery charger and was now dead.

Tears falling like raindrops, China silently prayed for a few seconds. The only other way to gain entry was walking in through a pedestrian gate. That is, if it wasn't locked. Her fears were deepened by the dead cell phone. Not even a flashing recharge warning came on.

An even deeper fear set in on China. If she got in through the gate she'd have to walk a ways to the reception building. It was quite a distance. She once again resigned herself to doing whatever it took to see Zaire.

Determination had won out.

Getting out of the car, China headed for the pedestrian gate. One hard push with her hand proved it was locked. She desperately considered climbing over. Tearfully, she conceded defeat. Wiping her eyes with the heels of her hands, she began the short journey back to her car.

China hadn't yet decided what to do when high beams lit up the car's interior. Turning around, she looked down the roadway, nearly blinded by bright lights. Making the decision to flag down the driver was a bit scary, but she could pull in right behind the vehicle if it got through. If it was an employee, they might recognize her as a guest.

Taking on the risk, China strode into the road, waving her hands back and forth. As the vehicle got closer, her heart sank. Her hands began to tremble.

Zaire braked hard, pulling his SUV roadside. Rushing

out of the car, he ran over to China. "I just recognized your car. It scared me to death. What happened? Are you out of gas?"

Shaking her head, China looked embarrassed and felt ashamed. "I have gas. I couldn't get through the gates. They wouldn't open. I parked and tried the pedestrian gate. It was locked."

Zaire scratched his head. "Where are you coming from this time of night?"

Exasperation setting in, China rolled her eyes. "I could ask you the same question. I haven't heard a word from you. Why've you been avoiding me?"

Looking puzzled, Zaire shrugged. "I haven't been. I came to the cabin after I left the pavilion. You didn't come to the door. I tried calling several times and got no answer. I figured you didn't want to be bothered. It hurt, China, real bad, so I didn't leave messages." He shook his head. "Listen, get in your car and follow me in. Is it okay to go to the cabin with you, where we can sit down and talk?"

All China could do was nod. If she spoke, she felt her voice would crack. She hadn't been this stressed-out in a long while. In fact, she'd been anything but stressed since she'd come to this idyllic place. Zaire had seen to that.

Putting his arm under China's elbow, Zaire directed her to her vehicle. Opening the door, he made sure she was all buckled in before he went back to his.

The gates opened a second after Zaire hit a remote button. A few minutes later, China and Zaire parked their automobiles in the spots nearest her cabin.

Wondering how to retrieve two keys from under the mat without Zaire seeing it had China on pins and needles. Breaking into a run, she nearly leapt onto the porch. She grabbed the keys, then closed them up in her hand.

China waited for Zaire to make it over to her. Panic hit

again. The cabin was empty, devoid of anything to suggest she'd ever been there…and she'd have to explain.

There was no way to let him inside and not explain its emptiness. The truth stared her in the face.

Taking the cabin keys from China's hand, Zaire opened the door. Stepping inside he flipped on the light, holding the door for her to enter.

As Zaire moved about the cabin, he mentally noted the differences. He looked at her. "What's happened in here?" He paused. "Don't answer that. Let's sit down and talk first."

"Let's do that." China was much calmer. "Care for something to drink?"

"No, thank you." Zaire sat on the sofa. "Let me say this before we get into us. Hailey's baby was born. She and Zurich have a son, delivered a couple of hours ago. That was one of several times I tried to call you and got no answer."

Deep joy filled her heart but she was sorry she hadn't heard the phone or Zaire's knocks. She had been in and out. Worn out from worrying, she'd later fallen into a deep sleep. She wouldn't insult him with details. Knowing what he'd already been through, she wouldn't have ignored him. China wasn't mean spirited by nature.

Dropping down onto a chair, China's eyes gleamed. "I'm so happy for them. Is he healthy? What's the baby's name? How much did he weigh?"

Zaire smiled. "Zurich Kingdom II is very healthy at nine pounds." He saw China's eyes widen with surprise. "Yeah, nine pounds. Mommy and son are fine. The new parents are so proud. We all are. We won't even talk about doting, joyous grandparents of a first grandchild."

"Thanks for the great news. As for our talk, do you mind if I go first?"

Zaire eyed her closely. "It's okay with me."

China's heart began to sink. "I was leaving the ranch early, Zaire."

"Why?" he asked, though he'd figured as much.

China cleared her throat. "Let me tell you why. When I didn't hear from you, I thought you'd turned the page. You believed I had grilled folks about your past and I'd done no such thing. We could get into Gayle's antics, but this conversation is about us. My mind was so tired and confused and I made a rash decision."

"You were outside the gates because you were leaving me?"

"I had left you in my mind. Everything is packed in the trunk. I didn't think you wanted me. I stopped outside the gates to look over this magnificent place and ponder us. Back in the car, I knew I had to see you and face down fate. I told you I loved you. My feelings haven't changed a bit. I know I'll come to love you more and more each day. I came to the conclusion I had no future if you weren't in it. That is, not a happy one."

The silence was almost tangible as he stared at China. Her nerves jangled so loud she wondered if Zaire could hear the rattling. Every part of her body was trembling. He'd either understand what she'd said and done or he wouldn't. She prayed for understanding.

Zaire got to his feet. It wasn't until he exited the cabin that China leapt out of the chair and started after him. The door closed just as she reached it. Looking helpless, she stared at the inanimate object between her and Zaire.

Falling to her knees, China sobbed hard. Coming back was all for nothing, yet she'd done the right thing by facing him. He was owed that much. They both deserved to speak their minds.

Getting up from her knees, China stretched out on the

sofa, deciding she'd leave at first light. She'd sleep here instead of the bedroom, where the sweetest memories of her and Zaire would be haunting.

Hearing a key in the lock, China looked up. Glancing at the table where Zaire had laid the keys, she saw one was missing. He hadn't used his master key, yet she hadn't seen him pick up hers. Eyes wide with trepidation, not knowing what to expect from him, China sat upright.

Dropping down on the sofa next to China, Zaire took her hand. "I had to get something important from the car. It's my turn. You poured your heart out, letting me know you'd left because you didn't think I wanted you. How you could've thought that, I'll never know. I've been honest about my feelings for you from the start. China, I'm so in love with you, I can't see straight at times. Your face constantly looms in front of me when I'm alone. I'm no good until I'm back in your arms. Tell me what you want to do. Where do you want us to go from here?"

China laced together her fingers. "For a while, I didn't know for sure what I wanted for us. The last hours were pure hell for me. I've missed you more than I knew was possible. I even wondered if Dad had found in you the man he'd love to have as a son-in-law. He'd want me to find love on my own, but he wouldn't hesitate to steer me onto the right path. I love you, Zaire. I want to be with you. I want to see if we can make it work. You and I can visit each other's homes while we figure it all out."

"Are…" He trailed off purposely. He wasn't going to insult her by asking her if she was sure, not after she'd poured her heart out to him for a second time in one night. He'd give her credit for knowing her own mind.

Zaire dropped down on his knees in front of China. Taking something from his pocket, he flipped the lid on a red velvet box, revealing a dainty promise ring. A solitaire diamond was adorned on each side by heart-shaped diamond chips. The platinum ring was beautiful.

"I give this ring to you as a promise to work through our issues, whatever they are and for however long it might take. I promise to be faithful while we figure it all out. You're a special woman and I'd hate for us to go our separate ways without seeing where we can go together. I want to be your best friend. Maybe someday I'll be your husband and father of our children. While that's being determined, we'll see each other here and in L.A. I want you to take time in deciding whether to make Texas home, China."

China looked shell-shocked. As she threw her arms around his neck, tears spilled over onto her cheeks. "Yes, Zaire Kingdom, yes," she cried out. "I promise to be faithful to us as we try and see if we're a good fit. You're in my blood. I don't want to try living my life without you if it can work with you. We've only known each other a short time, but I stand true to me and to my heart. And I'll be true blue to you. I love you."

Still on his knees, Zaire pulled China down to him, kissing her tenderly, passionately. There was no doubt in his mind what he wanted. This was the perfect woman for him. China Braxton was the only woman in the world for him.

Pushing China's hair back, he kissed her forehead. "I love you, too. Come home with me. We have lots of plans to make."

"Important plans! I can barely wait for us to get started." Cupping Zaire's face in her hands and closing her eyes, she kissed him fervently.

Thrilled over the countless blessings and good fortune bestowed upon them, the happy couple sealed their heartfelt promises with a long, breathless kiss.

* * * * *

Come away with me...

All I Want is YOU

Favorite author
DARA GIRARD

All I Want is YOU

DARA GIRARD

Beautiful and mysterious, Monica Dupree was once the envy of women and the secret desire of men. But now she lives a quiet life far from the limelight. Her safe haven is threatened when JD, a suave and seductive millionaire, sweeps her away to an island retreat in a sensual fantasy come true....

KIMANI
HOTTIES
✳ **MARRYING THE MILLIONAIRE** ✳

It's All About Our Men

*Coming in October 2011
wherever books are sold.*

KIMANI™
ROMANCE

www.kimanipress.com

KPDG2311011

REQUEST YOUR FREE BOOKS!

2 FREE NOVELS
PLUS 2 *FREE GIFTS!*

KIMANI™
ROMANCE

Love's ultimate destination!

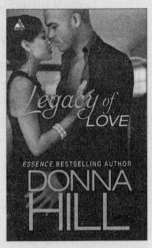